Grinder

RICHARD QUARRY

ALSO BY RICHARD QUARRY

THE EVOLVED SERIES:
The Big Empty
Point of No Return
The Outcasts
The Evolved
Holobrain
Grinder
The God Machine

The Further Tales of Odysseus:
Man of Many Turnings
Odysseus and the Eye of Odin

The Dance of Light and Dark
Dance of Sword and Heron
Dance of Deer and Shadow
Dance of Cat and Amber
Dance of Wolf and Moon
Dance of Ring and Dragon

Stand-alones

Absent From Felicity
Geneslide
Blue Dread
Trade All My Tomorrows
What Rough Beast
Midnight Choir

Collections:

Soldier of Discontent and other stories
Lord Under London and other cases of Nat Frayne
The Dread Men and other cases of Nat Frayne
Questing Song and other stories
Devolution Day and other f&sf stories

Chapter 1

First he remembered falling into the sun.

The blazing furnace of creation, searing out his eyes in one glorious explosion of light. Dancing jagged along every nerve in his body, laying bare the soul of the universe.

The clear white light.

His last thought. Almost.

But just as his body disintegrated and the radiation scrambled his neurons he called out....

ARVADA.

Chapter 2

ARVADA!

What?

He floundered into consciousness, peering through his mind for associations to give the name form.

But everything around him was black. Perhaps not impenetrable, but there was nothing to see.

He tried to grope around to establish his bearings. There was nothing to grip. Nor did he perceive any hands to grip with. He was disembodied; he could not feel himself occupying any space at all.

Only the name held clear.

Arva—

PAIN!

Blazing, searing pain.

The Sun! He must still be falling into the Sun!

He writhed, or tried to. But his body had been taken from him. Instead of tortured flesh, it was his nerve endings that spasmed to the mix of electric shock and bubbling white-hot flame. Nerve endings somehow thrashing throughout the body he no longer possessed.

He tried to scream. But, being bodiless, he could not invoke even that barrier between himself and the pain.

Arvada!

That name, again.

What did it mean? He had to know. Maybe he could appeal to it. Beg for mercy. Make amends for some past offence.

But how could he plead when he had no voice?

His last muddled thought, before nothingness at last enveloped him, was that he had come to a whole new hell, beyond even his acquaintance.

***

ARVADA!

Awareness awoke to THE WORD. Instinctively he tried to fold into a ball against the PAIN he feared coming. Only to find once again he had no body to fold.

What was it, then, that could feel such agony?

He was far short of an answer when the PAIN hit.

***

OVER AND OVER THE WORD pursued him. Came crashing, roaring, drooling down with demonic fury. He tried to cry, tried to whimper. But these were denied him. He had no mouth with which to sob, no eyes with which to spill tears.

And still THE WORD would not let him go.

Arva—

PAIN.

***

ONCE MORE HE CAME aware.

Instantly he tried to bar out THE WORD. But it dodged around his mental block and pursued him like a heat-seeking missile, turning and twisting to match his every mental dodge.

Somehow he knew that should he keep trying to lose his pursuer (don't name it!) by seizing on successive ideas, it would run him down. The forbidden thought was faster, more agile, more persistent. Besides, few ideas came to mind; it was as if a brush had scrubbed all thoughts from this mind.

So he tried to hide in a place he vaguely remembered, low down in his belly.

It wasn't there. No more than the rest of him.

THE WORD sprang up before him, coiled like a snake..

No!

In a last desperate effort he sought shelter within the center of awareness itself, the thinking-place. Though not so steady as ... (*something else*), it sometimes served as refuge.

He sensed the thinking-place inside him; a slightly lighter area in the dark. He plunged inside. Held imaginary hands to imaginary ears to try and hold himself inside the area that defined itself as HIM.

Quiet.

For a moment he thought he might have escaped. With every bit of mental strength left to him he clung to his precarious cave.

I AM I AM I AM I....

I am what?

PAIN.

He had time for one shadowy thought before the spasms and the searing heat blew his mind from its moorings.

Could there be a consciousness at work here? Hopelessly cruel, yet even so sharing the bond of Being?

As the agony began to burn away all effort to order his mind he made one desperate plea to that bond.

Please. Oh please. For the mercy of the sun, please. Free me from this torment named....

ARVADA

Chapter 3

THE EVOLVED LINE-OF-BATTLE SHIP drove its plow-like nose through the solar flares as it raced on a shrinking tangent toward the sun. Waves of heat, solar particles, and gravity V'd out behind it.

Hugging the wake, six fast cruisers of the Peregrine Alliance danced close as they dared about the larger ship. This deep down the solar atmosphere was thick enough that a strong buffet could throw a cruiser into a spin that would tear it apart.

But they had to stay close. Soon the giant ship must make its Jump. When it did, they had to enclose themselves in the same columnar section of grayspace that would carry them to its destination.

Closest of all clung the *Geirovar*. Belted tight in the Captain's chair, Arvada Sattar gave a mental command. The pigtail interface at the back of her neck transmitted the message through her helmet speakers.

"All ships, maintain Evasive Level 3. *Bhimadevi*, you're closing too far. Open another twenty kilometers."

"*Bhimadevi*. Acknowledged."

Communications both between and within the ships stayed sparse. Evasive Level 3 was violent enough on its own. Riding the edges of the Evolved's wake, with the star's gravity already dragging hard at every twist and turn, added to the strain.

Arvada heard the *Geirovar's* hull moaning, sometimes squealing with alternating compression and elongation. The engines, roaring at max thrust, gave off occasional staccato stutters, threatening to induce cavitations in the fuel flow. Should the engines cough out, they'd be hard as hell to re-start under this gravitation, with the ship sinking deeper toward its crush level every second.

But she had to keep up evasive maneuvers because the Evolved kept firing missiles. Radiation, long past the red zone for the Peregrine crews, gave the enemy sensors multiple vision. Even so, every now and then one burst close enough to rattle the ship. Setting off additional hiccups in the engines, and sending everyone's hearts into their throats if g-forces weren't already pulling them down into their bowels.

The atmosphere here was so thick with solar particles compressed by gravity it transmitted compression waves.

Aside from the tortured metal, the crew was enduring their own travails. Even with the inertial dampers at full strength and everyone aboard suited up to help pump the blood where it was needed and away from where it could rupture veins, Arvada felt like a water balloon bouncing downhill. With the bursting point not that far off, whether from ruptured organs or what felt like repeated punches to her head.

Thus she resorted to mental commands. Any sentence she tried to vocalize was bound to get squeezed off into a burst of gagging. Not the best way to soothe the wolf-pack's nerves.

"Stand ready," she cautioned the other five Captains. "She'll have to go into Jump soon."

The screens at the front of the semi-circular bridge showed Thais, the system sun of Harrar's Reach, spewing flares that even through the filters came harsh to eyes aching from the push-pull of evasive action. Gravitational fields superimposed in semi-transparent green over the white heat billowed up from below. Arvada didn't know how much more strain the Evolved ship could withstand, but her cruisers were right on the edge.

Jump, damn you, she urged the enemy. Much deeper and she'd have to call off the chase. The fast-shifting waves of heat, radiation, and gravitation were tossing the cruisers around like a storm at sea.

Everything depended on her ships, all her ships, enclosing themselves in the same segment of grayspace. Battle would cease as each separate vessel was swept along within the bizarre geometry of that netherworld. But coming out of Jump, it would take the ships of both sides some moments to fully materialize within the new area of space around whatever star the Evolved ship chose as her emergent point.

Theoretically, the fast cruisers, with their much lesser mass, should materialize faster.

As in, a few seconds.

Arvada would need all six of them to attack the much larger Evolved ship with any hope of success.

Would it work?

At least no evidence existed to prove it couldn't.

This was of course another of Sahan's wild-ass thought experiments. A roll of the dice that no one but Sahan Kotori would ever come up with, and no one but Arvada Sattar would ever dare try.

They'd made a damn good team.

Sahan. Her Sahan. Finally, after so many years, hers.

And then it ended, almost as soon as it began. With Sahan dead, and Arvada waking to a universe more lonely than she'd ever imagined could exist.

But in dying, Sahan destroyed the Evolved's Master Holobrain at Harrar's Reach. Now this single Evolved heavy had for whatever reason decided to make a break away from the Reach on its own.

At any odds, you couldn't ignore an opportunity like that.

By destroying the only Master Holobrain in Peregrine space, Sahan had done worse than shock the surviving Evolved out of their complacency. He'd terrified them. Should they now be killed, they would die alone. Which for the Evolved had unique and existentially horrifying implications.

The Terror Barrier.

And Arvada meant to keep it front and center in their minds that death was not anywhere near as unlikely as had first appeared when they decided to waltz into the Peregrine System. In fact she meant to make it downright probable.

If the Evolved folded, the navy still nominally loyal to the traitorous Commodore Raisa Catalan would melt away. They'd tried to pick the winner, but following Sahan's destruction of the *Elipida* torus, many sensed the tide changing. Another ill wind or two for the Evolved would have the Collaborationists flocking to the Alliance, gold-braided hats in hand.

Only those ill winds didn't blow out their cheeks all by themselves.

One small impediment was that Arvada herself was technically in a state of mutiny against her own Naval Command and Citizens' Council. In fact they'd declared her a War Criminal.

Criminal she might be, but at this point she wasn't just fighting the war. She *was* the war. And victory here would prove it.

So here she was, attempting a dubious tactic to defeat an Evolved heavy that in open combat would blow her cruisers out of space. It might yet get the chance.

She refused to acknowledge that revenge for Sahan might play any part in her decision.

Hate she could afford. Not vengeance.

Or so she told herself.

Chapter 4

He couldn't breathe.

Panic.

Memories of a malevolent figure grabbing him in the darkness. Of hands squeezing his throat, his head hammering for air.

But the hate and terror guiding those hands was absent.

He forced his mind to pull back from the vision. To feel out his situation, since all he could see was darkness.

The panic ebbed.

He still wasn't breathing. But he wasn't suffocating, either. An unpleasant sensation, but one that had been going on from the first.

He was alone.

Very alone. So alone that even his body seemed to have deserted him. He reached thought tendrils out searching for hands and legs. Found nothing. Instinctively he tried to raise his head to see if they were still there. Nothing happened. If he did have a head — he had to have a head, didn't he, you couldn't be aware without a head, couldn't be freaking *alive* without a head — no sensation registered to tell him whether he'd shifted or not.

He appealed to memory. And once again found nothing. Nothing except an equally bodiless flinch from something he could only identify as THE WORD. Whatever that was, and whatever it did. Ominous overtones sent his attention searching down new tracks.

He should have a name. Everyone had a name, like everyone had a head. Maybe if he could just get that far, other things would start falling into place. He strained after it.

It *had* to be there!

Nothing. Not even a hint.

That was unfortunate. Panic once more began to squeeze fingers around his throat. Trying to hold it at bay, he reached down within himself for ... something. Something that related to breath, he remembered that much.

It wasn't there. Nothing was there. Nothing was anywhere. *SHIT!*

He felt it coming for him. Terror. Loneliness so corrosive as to strip away your very soul. The long, long, panicked fall through the void.

Why could he recall nothing but the horror?

No place to hide. No limbs with which to fight. And no place left to make a stand, facing the threats arrayed against him while shorn of his last-ditch weapon, breath.

Except for one.

His mind. His attention. Pure concentration on the single fact of existence.

He shrank his awareness into a ball, a cavern echoing within his brain, with his missing eyes as the opening over which he drew a gray curtain. Though he felt fear whistling like a shrill wind outside, he held it at bay.

He knew this place. He'd deliberately cultivated it, made it part of himself. Not such a dependable refuge as ... (the *dan tien*, suddenly came to him, but what that meant he had no idea.) If only the storm of fear searching for cracks in the cave walls did not last too long, he could shelter here.

Shelter. Shelter. Shelter.

That one concept he permitted himself.

Shelter.

Time was lost to him. Shelter. The cavern walls started shifting in place. *Shelter.* Words and ideas pressed at him from outside.

Shelter, shelter, shelter.

Then THE WORD appeared. Crawling around — *shelter* — the walls of the cave. Snuffling like a hungry beast.

SHELTER!

Breath! He needed breath! You couldn't maintain such a state of one-pointedness without—

ARVADA.

PAIN.

And a long silent scream, for he had no throat and no breath with which to voice his agony.

***

EVENTUALLY, AWARENESS SOMETIMES CAME to him without the spasming agony of (careful!) THE WORD.

Not always. His first reaction on finding himself conscious was still to try to fold up in his non-existent body and whimper, mentally, as he braced for the PAIN. But sometimes THE WORD did not materialize.

Then portions of the darkness enclosing him gradually begin to take on a clouded suggestion of materiality. His awareness, floating disembodied, tried to infiltrate itself into these elusive pathways.

Eventually he hit on the idea of limbs, though the vague, numb boundaries were more suggestive of pseudopodia. Certainly they did not feel like limbs. Not even the leg he had lost.

What was that? Leg?

The memory pulled at him. He'd had a leg? And lost it? Where? How? Doing what?

Fragments came to him. Wreckage floating on all sides. Being pulled, funneled really, toward a rent in ... something. A huge structure, shattering into pieces — broken pieces of metal and broken pieces of bodies. They pressed in on him, all racing toward the vacuum of space, squeezing, squeezing. Then ... then....

Then he cried out for help. Cried out to....

ARVADA!

The PAIN crashed down on him.

His will had time for just one desperate cry before the pain ground it out:

WHY?

***

HE CAME OUT OF a long gray void to hear:

WHY? WHY? *WHY?*

The cries, his dying people's cries, dug deep into him.

Grinders pressed forward from above, from below, from all sides. Leaping from tripod to tripod behind waves of flares and streaking rockets and vibra-swords burning bright in infrared. The onslaught kept eroding his perimeter, one life at a time. The lives of his Marines and Riggers. They faced attack from more directions than they could possibly protect.

Screaming out their dying moments. Screaming in accusation, demanding or pleading to know why he'd led them into this trap.

WHY? WHY? *WHY?*

"Arvada!" he called on their private channel. "I need reinforcements! Right now!" Where was he? The Sector Seal aboard the *Enodia*, right. "We're surrounded. Send troops in from" — where? what were their dispositions? — "from Sector 2. We need to cut our way out of here while there are still any of us still left."

"Is that a considered battle report?" came her reply. No emotion but disdain for his panic. "You blunder into the Sector Seal with no reconnaissance, get yourself outnumbered and surrounded, and now you want to improvise battle plans? It might have escaped your memory, but while you've been off glory-hunting, I still have colonists to evacuate."

Colonists? What was the fucking situation? Why couldn't he remember?

WHY? WHY? *WHY?*

"You have a strike force in Sector 2!" he shouted. Come on, come on, come on, he urged her silently, we're down to minutes here. "There can't be any Grinders left there, they're all on us. Send them in. Quickly, before we're all massacred."

She was unmoved. Unbelievably so. "Commit my entire reserve to close-quarters combat, with no knowledge of enemy numbers except for your rather hysterical report? You are asking me to reinforce failure. Your failure. My clear duty is to rescue the colonists. When that is completed I will detach what forces I can to your assistance."

"We'll all be dead by then! My people!"

"Pull yourself together. If the situation is beyond recovery, try to die like a man."

"Arvada—"

"Sattar out."

But this was crazy. Arvada couldn't simply desert him this way. Did she *want* him to die?

Sahan stared around at the jackstraw maze surrounding him. The pyramidal beams cast triangular shadows in the sparkling light from Grinder flares. The enemy's insectoid armor gleamed yellow-green through the slanted lines of the struts. Everywhere he looked he saw masses of them crawling closer and closer. While his own people....

What had become of them? A moment ago they were still fighting. Now he saw only parts of them, sliced to pieces by Grinder blades. Sections of blue and white armor bounced off beams as they fell toward the torus floor, spiraling blood in their trail.

And yet ... no, no, it couldn't be. They weren't all dead. Torn to shreds by Grinder blades and Grinder teeth, some yet lived. Faces still in their helmets bounced around him, refusing to fall. They bore agony writ large in their expanded eyes, pulled-back lips, clenched teeth.

Dead. They had to be dead!

And yet....

They were talking. To him.

WHY?

"Arvada...." Help me. For Vishnu's sake, help me.

The Grinders closed in on him.

He heard himself whimper, hated himself for his own cowardice. No wonder Arvada wanted to be rid of him.

But then everything changed.

He was surrounded by debris, and it was all floating. Not toward the torus floor, where gravity-spin should take it, but *upward*. The support beams had torn loose, along with bits of machinery. And bodies, bodies everywhere, Peregrine and Grinders both, surrounded by bubbles of blood like tiny red fish.

He looked up. Through the sea of debris he saw a long rent in the hull, and beyond that, stars.

Hull breach! The omnipresent, suppressed terror of every habitat dweller.

Now the vacuum of space was pulling him upward along with the rest of the wreckage. The rent formed a funnel, squeezing the mass together. Bodies surrounded him, and pieces of bodies. Mostly his own Marines and Riggers.

Still screaming WHY? WHY? *WHY?*

Let me die. Please, just that. Let me go to them. Let me answer their accusations with my death.

But though he was squeezed and buffeted by the accusing heads, he did not die.

Instead he somehow made it through the breach in the hull to find himself floating in space.

Very crowded space. Debris and bodies, twisted sections of the torus hull and chunks of battered rock from the radiation shield ringed him round. Bouncing off each other like billiard balls, the smaller pieces caroming off the big ones at high velocity with no atmosphere to slow them down. Pulping bodies and bits of bodies in showers of red that instantly turned into ice crystals, shrouding him in a veil of crimson.

Yet the stars, the stars, they still shone above, almost close enough to reach.

Suddenly he no longer wanted to die.

He could turn on his suit transponder and Arvada could send a sled from the, the, the *Mettalise*, to haul him out of here before he got crushed. Tricky flying, but hardly impossible. He'd pilot a sled through this for one of his people, no question.

He turned on his transponder, then called Arvada on their private channel.

"I'm adrift in the debris field," he told her. "You should be able to pick up my transponder. Can you send a sled?"

"Are you kidding? In *that*?" Her voice held a sarcasm whose source he could not understand, but which withered him. "It's a suicide mission."

"I'd do it. You could do it." Why couldn't she understand? There was a bond of loyalty here. Whatever she thought of him, that bond should still hold.

"The torus is half gone," she said, "and the rest is breaking up as we speak. Priority is rescuing those colonists who have taken to escape pods. Sending a sled after you in that debris field would be throwing good lives after bad."

Good lives after bad? What the hell was she talking about? She couldn't just abandon him. Not after all they'd been through. No matter what she thought of him now, which he plain did not understand.

"Arvada—"

"Once we get the colonists safe, we'll see if there's any reasonable chance of retrieving you. Sattar out."

The line went dead.

He drifted, understanding none of it.

Arvada wanted him dead. That was the only possible explanation. Sahan knew he'd made himself something of a nuisance, but he thought he'd bottled up his feelings pretty good on the whole. And been loyal to a fault.

He loved her! She might not have wanted it, but knowing he'd devoted his whole heart and soul to her, how could she so callously abandon him to be ground to death?

One overriding mistake he'd made. That was to assume the woman had a heart.

Fool!

Some of the heads still wedged in their suits began whirling about with a good deal of velocity as they bounced off larger hunks of spinning debris. They came screaming at him.

WHY? WHY? *WHY?*

A helmet caromed off his leg, knocking him into a spin. Some torn and projecting section of the suit attachment tore a rent in his suit.

Breach!

Even as he thought it, the suit tourniquet irised shut. Right through his left thigh.

No, no, no! Arvada would never love him mutilated this way!

What are you babbling about? She left you here to die. If she could see, she'd be laughing. And you thought she might someday love you? Kali's balls, there's pathetic, there's bathetic, then there's Sahan Kotori.

Another spinning, screaming head tore a rent in his suit's right arm. The suit sealed the breach — *snip!* — just below his right shoulder.

Next came his right leg.

WHY? WHY? *WHY?* screamed the heads as they amputated more and more of him.

He twirled slowly, arms and legs gone but unable to bleed to death because the stumps were tourniqueted tight, and unable to die of shock because the suit injected chemicals to prevent it. Though they didn't ease the pain, which burned like fire where all four limbs had been.

And so he drifted, sobbing in shame and disgust at this travesty he had become. Yet even now he reached toward one word, and one only:

ARVADA.

Chapter 5

Arvada had foresworn revenge. Her task was victory.

Yet now as she pursued the Evolved ship, the *Geirovar* bucking and jibing, Arvada longed not just for victory, but slaughter. Her teeth ground together with the lust to cut Grinders into blood-spurting pieces. She groaned softly with the urge to plunge the living Evolved Captain within the ship she chased into the never-ending scream that Sahan called "the Terror Barrier."

Soon now.

Unless the Evolved ship was toying with them? Leading them so deep into Thais' atmosphere that the Peregrine cruisers would start to malfunction and perhaps sink to their doom, while it sped on unscathed?

Only one way to find out.

"Stand ready," she transmitted to her Captains one more time. "Remember. When we come out of Jump, you'll have at the most a few seconds to close on her. Once fully materialized, she'll blow us to pieces. Move in hard and fast. If you don't crumple some tin you're being too delicate."

Then it happened.

The squat Evolved ship with its sinking ram-like prow, so reminiscent of both a Greek trireme and a hard-shelled beetle, began to oscillate, just perceptibly.

A ruse? If she waited to make sure, her ships would overshoot beyond all hope of linking to the behemoth in grayspace.

"*Jump!*"

Her gorge rose to the familiar shuddery sensation. Her mind went hollow, shimmered back into awareness as the hull sang a discordant metal-tongued chorus, a wail suggestive less of distress than desolation.

Then they were there. The crew, Arvada among them, gave a collective sigh as the g-forces assailing their innards suddenly relaxed. The screens showed nothing because there was nothing to show. Literally. A drifting realm of *something*. Most of which did no more than scramble their sensors.

But concentrations of mass still registered.

"Captain," called Tarika Okada, harnessed up in her position at the center of the platform running around the fore part of the bridge. "She's in here with us. The Evolved ship. Can't be anything else."

"And our cruisers?" Arvada still used mental commands, rendering her voice slightly tinny in the speakers.

"Their signatures are blurred by such a concentration of mass. I'm pretty sure of two. And another possible. If the other two are on the far side of the Evolved ship, we won't see them."

And if they weren't there, the chances of successfully boarding the enemy declined by a third.

"Thank you, Nav. Captain LeFleur!"

"Here, Captain," replied the head of marines aboard the *Geirovar*.

His picture came through on the main screen of the swing-out console facing Arvada. He wore the full blue fighting suit of the Marines, complete with jetpacs in case the Evolved cut inertial damping aboard their ship. His bubble helmet bristled with small sensors, many of them doubled or tripled to withstand damage. The sensors would appear to interfere with peripheral vision, but the fighters would rely more on their sensors' than straight-line visual perception.

Standing behind the Marines in the cargo bay were over two hundred white-suited Riggers. Arvada and Sahan had pioneered the use of these volunteers in close combat. Though their mental integration with their suits was limited to infrared, magnetic, and radar, the suits of both Marines and Riggers were logarithmically boosted to similar power. What the Riggers lacked in specialized combat training, most more than made up for through practical experience in using the suits in space.

"All ready?" asked Arvada.

"Ready, Captain," said LeFleur.

Arvada searched for words to hearten the troops, who she imagined must be getting a bit nervous right about now. Like her.

She just wasn't that inspirational Joan of Arc kind of leader.

"Right, people," she said. "In a few minutes we will board and take an Evolved line of battle ship. Something the Evolved never believed could happen. Well, they're learning about Peregrines the hard way. And we will keep making it harder and harder, till there are no more Evolved left in Peregrine space. Now let's go and cut our way through till the enemy is ours."

To her great surprise, cheering sounded over the speakers. Just relieving tension, of course. She felt like shouting too.

Damn, she wanted to kill somebody!

"Captain!" cried Tarika Okada and Ligea Romero simultaneously.

The *Geirovar* was back in the universe of stars and space. A glaring sun on one side of her, the great blue-gray cliff of the Evolved ship's hull on the other, dwarfing the cruiser. The cliff flickered, its mass taking longer to stabilize after reentry into conventional space. For perhaps a quarter of a second Arvada was overwhelmed by the sensation of being crushed between two immensities.

But she was already shouting orders.

"Fire breaching charges! Close on her hard!"

Streaks of flame shot away from the wing mounts. The *Geirovar* turned belly-to toward the Evolved. There came a flash, and portions of the gray cliff peeled inward in a sharp-pointed flower pattern around a black hole through which blew debris suddenly sucked into to vacuum.

"Lay us alongside, helm. Hard! Hard!"

Abruptly the cliff was right on top of them. The cruiser smashed into it belly down, throwing Arvada upward against the seat restraints. The crash echoed throughout the hull. Her Captain's concern for her ship sent a quick remorseful shudder through her at the impact even as she clicked open the restraints.

"Boarders away!"

On the forward screens she saw the *Bhimadevi* do a belly-flop into the Evolved ship so hard she bounced off again, the bottom of her hull showing rippled steel. Undeterred, she drove in again, and this time fixed in place.

"In after them!" shouted Arvada, hoping all six of the cruisers had managed to breach the enemy hull. She didn't know how many Grinders might be aboard or where they might be. However many, this battle was to victory or death. Should the attack fail, the Peregrine cruisers could never withdraw under the weight of fire the Evolved heavy would rain down on them.

She swung toward Ligea Romero in the XO's chair at her side.

"You have the helm."

Then running for the elevator, she rode it down to the cargo bay, to shove her way forward through the Riggers of the boarding party still funneling through the vast open door of the bay into the black cavity blown into the hull of the enemy.

Arvada knew her proper place was on the bridge, coordinating the attacking forces of the six cruisers. However, she'd unloaded that task onto Captain Dainworthy of the *Anata.* She simply had to spill some blood.

Sahan, she called to his restless memory. *You were the best. Always. But now see how I can kill.*

Chapter 6

At last he learned he had a name.

He heard it from Arvada's lips.

Arvada. Heart-breakingly beautiful, heart-breakingly cold.

(Beautiful? A handsome woman, certainly. But his attraction — his obsession — had never been over her beauty. Now, though, he gazed in wonder at this cathedral of a women. A supernova bursting into realms of beauty and splendor hitherto unimagined. So his heart insisted. Yet his eyes could not quite assemble the full glorious picture.)

They stood in the landing bay of the *Viveca*. He did not recall how he got there. When he first saw her he flinched. Violently; half raising his arm to shield himself from a blow. He didn't know why. She'd hurt him so often, his heart had long ago lost its flinch reflex.

Now the sight of her filled him with dread.

Duncan Mallory stood at her side. The Earthman. Why wasn't he suited up? Hadn't he volunteered for this forlorn hope of a mission? All they needed was a body in the cockpit of the silver hunter-killer pointing like a spear at the hangar bay doors. Mallory could fly; he didn't need to think.

But Mallory should be in a suit. Not that any situation in which he might really need one wouldn't kill him. But it could add a boost to the inertial dampers trying to regularize the blood flow as the craft threw itself about space with Evolved missiles sniffing out its tailpipe like dogs chasing a bitch in heat.

Like Mallory chasing Arvada.

Correction, he reminded himself. Chasing no longer. The Earther had caught her, several weeks ago. The whole ship was full of it. Sniggering whenever (ah, his name, his name! embarrassing, to forget a thing like that) turned his back.

God, that hurt! Even for Arvada. This one cut deep, then twisted.

But what were they all doing here?

"Suit up, Sahan," said Arvada. Staring straight at him, contempt in her eyes. "You're going to fly this one."

Sa*han*, yes! Sahan ... Sahan Kotori. He *knew* it would come to him.

"But...." Take it slow. You're not at your best. "But didn't Mallory volunteer? This is his mission."

"I need him," Arvada told him. "More than I need you. You've turned into nothing more than a nuisance. Look at you, you can't even remember you own name. Now suit up and strap in."

No. No, this was crazy. He *knew* Duncan Mallory was slated to fly. The news had left him elated. Almost certainly the Earther would be killed attacking ... whatever the target was. Of course if he did survive he'd return a hero. But —Sahan, Sahan Kotori dammit, sharpen up — had nothing to lose. Any chance he ever had for Arvada had long since withered and died. His hope had learned to feed on ashes.

"I said suit up," Arvada repeated. "Or fly without. I don't care. Just do it now."

Sahan tried to protest, found nothing to say. Nothing made any sense. Had he forgotten something again? His mind, his mind ... was not always to be trusted. And Arvada was such a distraction.

Wait! Now he had it. Mallory *had* volunteered. Only he never meant to go. Instead he and Arvada lured Sahan (ha, got it the first time!) into the hangar bay. They'd make him fly the mission, then report that Mallory had stubbed his toe or something and had to be replaced. Sahan wouldn't be in any position to contradict their story. He'd be dead.

It made sense, and yet....

He stared around. He knew he was in the hangar bay. The hunter-killer gleamed right there before him. But everything else ... he had a vague impression of machinery, of a vast semi-cylindrical room, of other craft parked nearby. He could see them. Sort of. Only every time he tried to actually focus on anything, the surroundings turned all vague and cloudy.

And Arvada. Black hair, honey-colored eyes. It was her alright, but ... too glaring to actually make out her features. As if made out of glass, not skin, with a light shining through it from behind.

This was wrong. All of it. Just wrong.

"No," he told Arvada. "I'm not going."

PAIN.

"Stop *twitching*!" she snapped.

The pain stopped, leaving him ashamed at his show of weakness. Frightened, too, with a fear that hovered over him like a carrion bird.

And hurt. The ache pulled at his heart, causing it to stumble over itself. He struggled to breathe.

Arvada meant to kill him. His hapless love had finally lost its amusement value. He'd become no more than an annoyance, and Arvada would no longer suffer him to live in her world.

"I'm through waiting, Sahan," she told him. "Get in the cockpit. Now. You can go with whatever show of dignity you can still scrape up, or you can go bloody and whimpering. But you're going."

Sudden anger wisped his mind into whirlpools.

"*No!*" he screamed. Bloody and whimpering? We'd see who ended up bloody. He was Sahan Kotori, and ... and for some reason, that should make him formidable.

He flew straight at her.

But again something was wrong.

Arvada did not bother to evade his charge. Instead she punched him in the face, then the ribs, the blows coming so fast he never even began a defense. Then grabbing his shoulders as he reeled breathless and confused, she swept him around and hurled him into a piece of machinery three meters away. His feet never touched the ground till he bounced off and landed in a heap.

This time he felt no pain. Instead a form of paralysis came over him.

This is wrong, he kept repeating, and though his conviction never wavered, the meaning did. Was it wrong because Arvada had no right to betray him this way? Or wrong because the whole situation was somehow just ... wrong?

Tossing him over her shoulder — she'd always been strong, but he marveled that she handled his limp weight so effortlessly — Arvada mounted the ladder to the open cockpit of the hunter-killer. There she slung him into the pilot's seat. Leaning over, she touched a button on the arm and the restraints slid together and clicked into place.

"Arvada...." But he had no argument to make beyond "please." And he knew what that would get him.

"Oh, stop blubbering. I can't stand you always underfoot all the time, looking like a puppy that's just been kicked. You should thank me. I've finally found something useful for you to do."

She slammed the cockpit shut. The engines were thrumming — he didn't remember hearing ignition — and the autopilot was engaged. Arvada and Mallory must have made record time clearing the hanger bay, because the half-moon door of the exit irised open. The hunter-killer rolled forward.

Sahan tried first to disengage the autopilot, then to override it using the manual controls. Everything he touched went inert.

"Wait!" he shouted toward the radio, though it was unlit and silent. "Where am I going? What am I supposed to do?"

Die, came the answer deep in his head, and he saw Arvada's smirking face behind it. Just die. Even you should be able to manage that.

The hunter-killer soared out from the lights of the hangar deck into the darkness beyond. Acceleration pinned Sahan back in his seat, leaving him just enough breath for one final cry:

ARVADA!

Chapter 7

Had the Evolved anticipated that one of their ships might be boarded?

The idea seemed incredible to Arvada Sattar. Since the one-sided rout at Demeter the Evolved had shown nothing but contempt for Peregrine capabilities. Though Sahan gave them a jolt by invading the holobrains to fight the Evolved — and win — Arvada's victories had come against other Peregrine ships fighting for the traitor Catalan.

Yet now her boarding parties were running up against tactics apparently designed to counter them. The first, of course, were waves of Grinders, as expected.

The second was to shut down visual.

The Evolved did this through the simple mechanism of rapidly strobing lights. The first sense Riggers and Marines learned to integrate through their brain implants and sensor interface was vision. With experience they could take in 360 degrees, perceiving a coordinated picture in the center of their heads, though one quadrant always remained dominant. The flashing lights brought on a shuffling-card discontinuity that induced high-frequency brain waves that interfered with the formation of coherent images.

How the Evolved generated such lights was unknown. From the reports of the other boarding parties, they appeared to be operating over the entire ship.

This left the Peregrines reliant on sensor inputs of infrared, radar, echo location, and motion detection. They'd all, even the Riggers, trained to function without visual. But what training could prepare you for a shifting welter of colors behind which came a vibra-blade and crunching alloy teeth?

Of course the Grinders suffered the same limitation. But they rushed forward screeching and clattering, seemingly heedless of their lives. In these conditions tactical finesse too often degenerated into simple smashing and hacking, the only defense a fixed purpose of murder.

Arvada, with her own blood lust bubbling well over the rim, realized this early on. Yet how could she tell others, beyond yelling "cut, cut! Cut them down!" into her speakers?

She didn't have much time for essay construction. All six boarding parties reported the same: the Grinders kept falling back behind a regular series of counter-attacks. They quickly abandoned any open expanses within the Evolved ship that would give the advantage to the Marines' shoulder weapons. They they'd cling like barnacles in the close-quarters areas of the ship, where the struggle came down to a front line of half a dozen Peregrines chopping away at a similar number of Grinders, both sides shuffling in fresh bodies over the corpses, and any advance possible only by literally cutting a wall through the opposition. Here progress dragged along meter by bloody meter.

With some trepidation, Arvada divided up her boarding party from the *Geirovar* in order to attack along a broader front. She ordered the other commanders, in some cases over their protests, to do the same. This risked one of the smaller forces getting flanked and overwhelmed by superior numbers, but was the only way to make any real progress toward their target, the bridge of the Evolved ship.

Because if another Evolved ship came through the Jump point, or even a handful of Catalan's cruisers, Arvada would lose her ships and find herself trapped here.

She soon realized the only strategy possible was attrition. Regrettable, but necessary. With all six cruisers locked onto the Evolved hull, she had close to a thousand troops fighting their way through the corridors, half of them Marines. From her previous experience of being boarded by an Evolved heavy, she estimated the Grinders would number somewhere around six hundred.

Experience had also taught her that the Marines would achieve a positive kill ratio against the Grinders, and the Riggers break even at the very least.

On the other hand, the close terrain favored the defenders.

Impatience and worry, plus a hunger for that very revenge she'd renounced, kept driving her forward into the front line, despite all pleas from the troops for her to stay back.

It was a vicious place, there on the sharp end. As the two lines of fighters squared off in a corridor, there was little time to orient yourself. Arvada had just stepped to the front to replace a fallen Marine when a whirlwind depicted by radar in vivid emerald-green came straight at her, surrounded by a ghostly aura of infrared.

Her immediate reaction was something along the lines of, *shit!* But training and anger were already coming into play as she identified the specter's raised weapon by its brighter infrared signature. With Marines hemming her in on either side, she lunged forward beneath the descending vibra-sword, twisting into a shoulder strike.

The impact of the two powered suits smashing together caused her head to overshoot her neck, producing a spiking pain she did not register and a brief sense of displacement from the shock. But hers was the more coordinated and better grounded movement. The Grinder bounced off, his downward stroke produced no more than his forearms banging off her suit. As he recovered his balance, raising his sword for another strike, she followed through the shoulder strike with an upward-ripping backhand stroke of her battle-saw. She heard blood splatter her helmet as the Grinder's insides, marked in a sudden flowering of infrared, gushed through the rent in his suit. As he fell Arvada saw another quick splash of infrared from his helmet, where she guessed his skull had just exploded.

Now being a half-step in front of the Peregrine line, she planted herself in place, willing the others forward. The ghostly green-and-red outlines of Grinders wavered like breeze-ruffled flags on either side of her. If they even perceived Arvada in their sensors' peripheral vision — adrenalin shrank one's visual field down close to a straight line in combat — they were too preoccupied with foes to their front to strike at her.

For all her training in simulated combat with visual shut down, Arvada still found it a strange and intimidating sensation to be assailed by billowing apparitions of green suffused with dull red, with a hint of trailing yellow from echo location.

One of the Grinders to her front jerked his dead companion back to clear a space. Then he and another came swinging their swords at her from the left and right quadrant at the same time.

Hemmed in on three sides, Arvada leapt in the only direction left to her. Straight between the two swords, with all the power of her suit. She came down planted at a forty-five degree angle in a jam of Grinders, milling rather than striking because there wasn't any room.

Too close for a battle-saw, too close for vibra-sword. Her angled posture was awkward, but did keep her below the level of the Grinders' teeth, though a jack-hammer clatter told her at least one was trying to chew through her helmet.

Arvada tried to grab her knife but her arm got pinned. There came several frantic seconds of pushing and swaying and desperate stamping in order not to be knocked off her feet. If any of the Grinders could get their own knives free, she was dead meat.

Then the silver field surrounding her turned to blue. The Marines, seeing their Captain launch herself into the press of Grinders, followed after with complete abandon. Knocked back by main force, the Grinders grabbed at each other trying to get their feet planted, more often than not defeating their own purpose. Though individually brave/crazy, the Grinders were never skilled at group maneuvers.

The Marines washed over their stumbling foes like a bloody wave.

Later this too would become part of the Arvada Sattar legend, how she broke a close-quarters stalemate in the corridor by powering straight through.

A mix of struggling, tight-packed Grinders, dead ones without room to fall, along with detached parts of them spurting blood, were shoved all the way down the halls. It was like cutting into a wall of meat. The Grinders gave screeches of frustration and howls of rage, along with cut-off staccato shouts. They rarely screamed, because any damage bad enough to cause such a reaction almost always exploded their heads into a streaky infrared soup.

So fast did the Marines push them that the Grinders never got a chance to regroup. Here and there one, or maybe two or three, would try to make a stand, only to be cut down immediately. The main factor slowing the Marines' charge was clearing a path through the bodies.

The Grinders could be ferocious fighters. But always they relied on sheer fury rather than tactics. So that when they found themselves in a tactically impossible situation, instead of adjusting to it, they most often fought and died where they stood.

As the Grinders raced down the corridors, some fighting, some fleeing, but totally disorganized in either case, Arvada thought victory had arrived.

Then she heard the explosions.

***

CAPTAIN SEVERIN OF THE *Mista* was first to call in on Arvada's private channel. "The Evolved are blowing up the ship!" he shouted.

Within less than a minute one other Captain and three First Officers leading assault parties from their ships broke in with the same urgent message.

Arvada could hear the explosions herself, dead ahead. Apparently the same thing was happening ahead of all the attacking parties.

Her first reaction was, not to put too fine a point on it, panic. Here was her chance to lose not only six fast cruisers, but a disproportionate number of the Marines and fighting Riggers available to the Alliance.

With that immediate reaction out of the way, she settled down.

"Everyone, listen to me. They aren't blowing up the ship."

"Sure sounds like they are," said Severin.

It sounded rather like that to Arvada too, as concussive balls of thunder rolled down on her, given a metallic edge by crumpling steel. An ominous echo persisted within the tight confines of the corridors. And though irrelevant to the problem at hand, the smell of blood crowding through her suit's filters added to the sense of doom. Suddenly her mouth was so dry it tried to stick together. She took a quick sip from her drinking tube.

"I have to believe," she told her group leaders, "that if the Evolved truly wanted to destroy this ship, they would have a quicker and more thorough way to do it."

There, that made sense. She was proud of herself. The mumblings transmitted to her auditory centers slowed and lost volume, though they did not cease.

"The Evolved aboard this ship," she told them, "doesn't want to die." That much she'd learned from Sahan. She still didn't understand everything he'd told her about the holobrains and the Terror Barrier, but that one central fact had lodged deep. "I know you don't necessarily understand this, but trust me. With the Master Holobrain destroyed, death is a greater horror to them than we can conceive of."

"So what are they doing?" Severin demanded.

Yes, what? Arvada took a look around, as best she could without visual. The corridors softly limned in green by radar vibrated just perceptibly from the force of the explosions booming all around. She could feel the vibrations travel upward through her feet. The Grinder bodies lying scattered ahead of her shuffled eerily along the floor like red and green worms.

"What if the Grinders are pulling back so they can blow up the areas we're in?" asked Jamaya Torhena, XO of the *Cressida*.

Thanks, I needed that. The alarmed voices crowding into the center of her head crescendoed. Only about half the officers had ever been in any real form of battle, and less than half of them had fought Grinders at close quarters.

That was it. The Evolved hoped to force the fighting even closer. To let the Grinders bring one of their most formidable weapons, their artificial jaws, into play.

She couldn't evacuate. She'd lose the cruisers and everyone aboard trying to escape the Evolved ship.

On the other hand, there was little chance the living Evolved would destroy the whole ship. Not while he was aboard. He'd surrender first.

And if his delaying tactics brought reinforcements?

Well that would just be one big pain in the ass. But Arvada thought that was: 1) unlikely; and 2) nothing she could do damn-all about anyway.

"Enough!" she shouted over her officers' increasingly loud projections of doom. "Everyone just settle down. Now here's what's happening. So far the explosions are relatively far away. My belief is that the Evolved running this ship is creating a final barrier between us and the holobrain. Tearing up the ship to force us to even closer quarters with the Grinders. They started to panic, this was the fallback plan. So we follow."

The voices mixing in her head fell far short of a stirring affirmation.

"Have the Marines leave off their jetpacs," she ordered.

Jamaya was unhappy. "But if the Evolved turn off inertial damping—"

"They won't. Not till we fight through the wreckage, anyway. The passages will be too cramped to risk getting wedged in. The Riggers following behind can carry the pacs." Until we have to send the poor bastards in. "Now we have a lot of nasty eyeball-to-eyeball fighting to do, so cinch it up. Okay, people. Move out."

"With me," she said to the Marines gathered around her. Further back down the corridor the white-suited Riggers waited, not having had a chance to enter the fighting yet. Stirring, mumbling, showing their restlessness and their fear. As Arvada started up the hall Marines quickly filtered around her to take the brunt of whatever they might run into.

Soon they came to the mass of wreckage left by the explosions.

"I hate this Mines of Moria shit," said one of the platoon leaders. Nervous laughter followed. Then the Marines began twisting, climbing, proning out to crawl, infiltrating themselves into whatever cavities offered.

Sahan, maybe I can never truly know what it was like for you in the Sector Seal of the *Enodia*. I hope not. But I'm getting closer.

Chapter 8

Over and over he tried manipulating these supposed limbs that had appeared out of the darkness.

Some things improved, slowly. Gradually he came to differentiate arms from legs, if only because enough of up and down had been restored to him that he recognized they lay in the appropriate place. Arms above, legs below. And four of them, distinctly four. Always a good sign. Six might have got him wondering.

Sometimes he dared tell himself that these limbs, independent-minded as they were, might actually be the originals. Which meant there might actually be more of him present than met the eye, did he have any eyes, and he might hope someday to crawl out from this dark tunnel.

Against that was an uneasy ... memory? More like a dream, blurry around the edges but becoming more solid as new bits and pieces emerged. And this dream kept hissing through all his attempts at denial that he had lost his real arms and legs in some past disaster.

But where?

ARVADA.

PAIN.

He quickly learned to avoid that line of thought.

Wherever these arms and legs came from, they would hardly have graced a classic statue. Instead of taut-drawn musculature, they appeared as wiry bundles of lines, in all colors but tending most prominently toward reds and yellows and purple. Within the lines lay no substance other than the general blackness, either in appearance or responsiveness. The lines tended toward a billowy sort of motion, even when the limbs themselves lay still as a stone.

His mind's connection to them was most tenuous. He tried to visualize them in his awareness, then from some memory or instinct direct them to move in a certain manner, to a certain place.

In response they waved, stirred about, then flopped into stillness. Only the most tenuous sensory signals came back to him. You could sever the bright lines with a cutting torch and he doubted he would feel a thing.

He found this most discouraging. Because for all he knew, this wavering Self he tried to cling to with indifferent success might be no more than a brain in a jar, and his putative arms and legs just skeleton limbs laid out on some table or hanging from a wall. They might be illuminated jellyfish, and their motions nothing to do with him at all.

Did he really have a Self? A previous life? He thought so, because sometimes he had bad dreams. Waking, though, he remembered only hints he dare not pursue, lest they lead to THE WORD.

Maybe this person, this life he hoped someday to reclaim, was after all nothing but a collection of cultured brain tissue, with all its life experience, if any, yet to happen.

Maybe it was a bunch of circuits, and the reason he had such trouble finding his Self was that he didn't have one. That *this* was as alive as this quantum-computer-that-dreamed-itself-a-man would ever get.

Such thoughts could get him despondent and sulking.

But no one cared.

So he might as well keep on striving. Not because he wanted to, not even because it would likely make a difference, but because even if he was a hamster on a wheel (where did that image come from?) and any idea of forward progress an illusion, running at least gave you some exercise.

If you had legs, of course.

And so he practiced with the four assemblages of bright lines constantly.

After ... who knew how long, he had no sense of time — he realized that his ability to control his limbs' movements with precise mental commands was not improving with practice. Yes, every now and then something occurred his over-eager mind construed as progress.

If he concentrated very hard on directing one of his arms to bend, for example, sooner or later it would bend — however far it wanted to. If he tried to direct the fuzzy projections he regarded as his hands toward a precise point in space ... they laughed at him. He'd do better trying to teach them rude gestures to taunt him with.

But he would have to master the whole lot if he was ever to return to the realm of....

People?

People?

That was the operative word.

Just what objective evidence did he have to prove he *was* a *people*?

What if the instincts and reflexes relevant to such organic ordering were not after all in his repertoire?

That was discouraging.

More than discouraging, actually.

In fact for a time it quite drove him mad.

Because as more of his memory filtered back, he realized there were a lot of qualities of *people* he lacked. Breathing and eating and motility to begin with.

Very well, he tried to tell himself, accidents happen. But if he was still at root *people*, they could also un-happen.

Up to a point.

And if he was past that point?

Vast chasms of fear and loneliness made him fold his mind up into a ball. Then try to squeeze so tight it would wink out of existence.

No luck. He continued to exist as a disembodied awareness floating in the dark. Loathing itself. Mentally screaming and sobbing and throwing himself at the walls of his cage and vowing that if he ever got loose he would destroy the entire universe.

Because for him personally, what would be the difference?

Of course hard as he tried, he couldn't really, literally, scream or sob. Or even breathe hard, come to that. Just rip in frustration at the fibers of his own mind.

Nor could he throw himself against the walls of his cage because he had no body to throw, and the "cage" was a dark void. And if anyone was coming to get him because he truly was a *people* after all, and the human community fully intended to retrieve him from this dark prison because that was what *people* did, they certainly were taking their own sweet time about it. Trying his faith, in fact.

Only he didn't really believe anyone was trying.

That despair lasted a long time.

Then sometime, somehow, he crawled up from the pit of terror and loneliness and self-loathing that defined his existence. Partway.

The way he thought about it, he needed to achieve a lower resting state. That is, reorient himself to this whole concept of *people*. He might have *been* a *people*, once. Or he might be something created in a lab. He might be a prototype for a new generation of robots, and if any genuine *people* ever asked how he felt about it, he would do his mechanical best to pinch their breathing, talking, seeing head off. But for now he must temper all hopes of a future that might involve his reappearance as a *people*.

Since he still existed, through no fault or desire of his own, he better take whatever steps he could to actualize that existence. No matter how constrained.

Which meant mastering to whatever degree possible these wire-framed, parti-colored grotesqueries that must serve as limbs for a maybe-maybe-not-*people*.

And yet, the means he finally hit upon came directly from the realm of *people*.

He didn't know where. He had no memory of any such skill. Yet as he renewed his effort to establish communication with his distant limbs, a pattern of movement began to emerge.

A form of wave, actually. He no longer sent signals ordering his limbs to execute all the lifts and bends necessary to arrive at some pre-determined point. That never achieved anything but a lot of defiance and flopping around.

Some instinct made him send a mental wave into his right arm.

And it moved. The hand — a blur of colors, actually — went to the point he designated. Approximately.

Then collapsed, inert.

How had he done that?

A sort of mental expulsion. A visualization of a yellow sine wave projecting from ... from where his breath would have been anchored did he have any breath. An expulsion lacking its proper physical foundation, yet possessed of a definite if abstract form for all that. A form he had just infused into his heretofore-recalcitrant limb.

He tried moving his other limbs one at a time, projecting the same mental wave. They moved. Not precisely according to his intent, but a hell of a lot closer than anything he'd managed before.

After more practice, he tried moving them together. As in....

He wasn't sure. A dance.

How would he know about a thing like that?

Don't get diverted. Remember, THE WORD finds PAIN for wandering thoughts.

So, he danced. As best he could, as best he remembered. Expelling the intent of each move into his arms and legs. And lo and behold, they began to dance with him. In no more than a semi-coordinated fashion, true. Not enough to give him some clue what form of dance he was attempting.

Yet he was elated. For he believed a pattern nonetheless existed, pulling toward some larger whole. Someday, *someday*, it would reveal itself.

On that point he was determined.

Meanwhile, he still had the glory of movement, after being immured within the confines of his disembodied awareness for so long.

As he danced his perception of his limbs began to alter. Instead of mere lines, his arms and legs appeared to trail banners, or flowing silk cloths, delicate as the undulating fins of some tropical fish. And the patterns they formed in all their waving colors ... implied something profound.

Waiting for him.

Chapter 9

IT WAS A MORASS. A jumble of twisted walls and jagged-toothed steel and dangling wires and blown-open machinery scattering parts of unknown function.

Grinders and Marines slithered through the metallic swamp. Fighting close as animals, bloody and primitive as animals, and in the case of the Grinders, even with the same weapons as animals; their chittering external jaws. For both sides animal tactics prevailed; ambush, followed by frenzied violence.

The Grinders excelled at this type of fighting. However, it was by now coming clear that they were in fact outnumbered, just as Arvada had hoped. But far from resigned. Within the maze of wreckage left by the explosions, the Peregrines could not concentrate and exploit their superior numbers. Crawling through the tiny passages you could see the heels of your comrades ahead of you as they fought for their lives, and still be unable to do a thing about it.

Despite appeals from her own Marines and the other group leaders, Arvada crawled right alongside the others into the now amorphous killing zone. Since the flaring lights that previously blocked visual couldn't function amid the wreckage, she had visual back. Big deal. There was no external lighting to see by, and she sure as hell wasn't going to send any Grinders a formal challenge by shining on her lamps. Line of sight never reached beyond four meters anyway, and with the tortured roofs, floors, and walls bulging in and out like a fractious sea, most often less.

So she crawled along, occasionally rising to a crouch, now and then even standing in narrow pockets, trying to make sense of the multitudinous green shadings radar depicted around and ahead of her. Echo location added curves and angles of yellow, but within such a small and chewed-up field, its main effect was to add a ghostly haze to the landscape. Arvada only kept it on because it might alert her more quickly if some Grinder suddenly materialized out of the maze of green lines and curves and planes through which she cautiously made her way.

She crawled up and down small hills of debris, peering into the green murk. A hunter, hunting for infrared. Though she tried to spot and work around them, shards of metal sticking up from the broken floor could not entirely be avoided. Hooking her suit, they tried to hold her back. Delicately she worked her way free. The suits could resist rough usage; by the same token, if she used the full power of the suit to rip free of some particularly pernicious metal thorn, that degree of force might open a breach. The Grinders, or the Evolved, had not evacuated the atmosphere yet, but Arvada didn't want to be stranded deep in the ship with a rent suit if they did. Should the ship be opened to space and the temperature plunge toward absolute zero, the suit would seal the breach by any means necessary short of cutting your head off. As at the *Enodia* it had sealed the breach in Sahan's suit by amputating his leg.

She crawled under a leaning beam, shoving her battle-saw before her in her right hand while keeping her knife folded back along her left wrist. Beyond the beam a ragged curtain of torn electrical wires dangled. Cautiously she reached out with the saw. A shower of sparks erupted in the darkness. To whom it may concern. Great.

She could wriggle back out, hoping no Grinder had slipped in behind her, and try to find another route around the wires. Arvada knew there were Marines to either side of her, plus many more behind and likely a few in front. But she couldn't see them. The passage she'd started down left her isolated on all sides.

Backing out would not be dignified.

The floor ahead looked broken up, but sufficiently thick with debris that she did not expect some ambusher to erupt suddenly beneath her. Ahead, just beyond the dangling wires, the roof bulged down to within a meter of the floor. The Evolved alloys showed great ability to bend and distort without shattering.

The sides of the little cave were more problematic. A jumble of green lines thick as a tangle of bamboo. What anchored them, and how solidly, she could not tell. Foolish to expect she'd be safe from attack on either side. What Arvada most definitely did *not* want was a Grinder on her back in such a tight space, trying to chew through the juncture of helmet and suit, and then onto her pigtail on its way to her vertebrae. What would that be like, to have your pigtail slowly mutilated? What sensations would shoot through your brain?

Not a lesson she wanted to learn.

But she detected no hint of infrared. Unless the Grinders had developed some brand-new technology since they last time they'd met in combat, their suits did a terrible job of suppressing heat signatures.

Why not take a break for lunch, while you're thinking about it?

Something was changing. Arvada could not tell just what. She seemed more internally agitated than she had a little while ago, even while playing cut-and-thrust with the Grinders.

Of course. You're frightened, and thinking too much about it.

Only she wasn't frightened. She was ... eager. A prickling urgency rising from her guts to tickle her heart. Almost sexual. More than almost. Like that moment when kissing was just wasting time.

Kill.

Her prey lay ahead.

Without further thought, Arvada undulated forward. Straight into the dangling wires.

Her suit shed the electric discharges, but the tiny chamber lit up in magnesium-bright showers of sparks that shattered the uniform blackness otherwise registering on visual. A glittering form of St. Elmo's Fire shimmered along the floor. A glow to alert any foe within ten meters.

She *smelled* it! Smelled the electricity! That shouldn't happen. She'd doused her pheromone detectors at the first of the fighting because the smell of blood added nausea to the sensations of doubt and dread already assailing her.

But now she could clearly smell the ozone in the air, right through her helmet's filters. She crawled quickly through the field of sparking wires, the ozone scent bringing to mind swimming through the *Kepler's* ocean with Sahan.

Sahan.

Vengeance.

Lust.

The Grinder hit her from above just as she cleared the wires and wiggled past the bowl-shaped depression in the roof.

The sudden glow of infrared gave half a second's warning; otherwise she would have had him on her back.

She didn't have time to swing her battle-saw up and around. Releasing the saw, she tried to spin, but only got halfway. The creature smashed into her right shoulder. Fortunately the maze above from which it dropped must have been too tight to allow for a vibra-sword, or she might be watching her blood fountain out right now.

As it was she had the Grinder sprawled across her right side, pinning her arm as it hugged her close with all the power of its suit. But as she spun Arvada used her bent legs to shoot forward half a meter, so the creature's auxiliary jaws did not reach her neck.

Instead it clamped its external mouth onto her shoulder and began chewing. A fast-pitched staccato clacking rose to a screeching whir as its alloy teeth skittered over her suit while she tried to shake it off. Incongruously, the probing teeth tickled her shoulder. The material would resist the Grinder's jaws for a time — seconds only; she wasn't sure how many.

Even with the beast's jaws whirring away in her ears and the prospect of losing an arm seconds away, Arvada was not frightened.

Angry, yes. But even more — or so she would come to think of it later — *hungry.*

In the flurry of actions that followed, Arvada had no impression of herself as Arvada Sattar, fighting for her life.

Or indeed of anything human at all. More like some predator flowing over its ancestral prey.

The Grinder was on top of her, holding her arms pinned, her left side digging into the shards of metal lining the floor. Bringing up one knee, Arvada tried to roll him hard backward into the floor. The Grinder splayed his legs wide to either side to hold his position. Reaching her right leg up through the opening, Arvada kicked off with all the power the suit would give her against the inverted dome of the roof.

They shot forward still locked together. Shards of the broken metal floor pulled at her suit. Several tore through, ripping her flesh beneath. These abruptly checked her momentum. The Grinder, with nothing but the toes of his boots touching the ground, flew forward. He managed to catch himself with his chest opposite her helmet. But his embracing arms were at such a downward angle she broke his grip with a mere flick of her arms.

Then brought the knife in her left hand up and around and plunged the whirring blade right through his suit.

He jerked. Holding him in place, Arvada worked the knife around in the cut. She saw his head explode, but kept on cutting.

By the time she stopped and rolled him away something that looked like a kidney plopped out of his suit, along with a lot of blood and some pieces of tissue she could not identify.

To her sudden shame, she found herself salivating.

Chapter 10

ON AND ON HE danced. Pushing waves out from his mind to inject animating energy into his arms and legs, uniting mind and body in one splendid whole. Wire-outlined limbs streamed semi-transparent colored banners out behind, wisping away as they trailed further into the darkness. Signaling some larger pattern he yearned after but could still not grasp.

Oh exultation. He could *move!*

Only within the darkness that still surrounded him, true.

Nor could he actually *feel* these movements. He felt the force of the waves emanating from his mind. But as the waves extended into his limbs they touched nothing.

Yet for all that, the waves and the impulses of a dance that generated them still provided a much more lively and accurate response than conscious direction had.

It would probably help if he could breathe. He ... not quite remembered, but had a sort of unfulfilled urge that strongly implied, that it was breath that generated true force to these mind waves. But that sensation was still denied him.

Too bad. Because his newfound facility of movement had him pretty well convinced that he was a *people* after all. *People* moved. Like him. They didn't just sit around in the darkness dreading the next occurrence of (careful, careful) THE WORD.

On the other hand, *people* also breathed. In fact he rather thought they numbered breathing high among their achievements.

But it did not do to cavil. Doubt led to depression. Depression led to retreat. To winding himself up in his little ball like — like some animal or other he could not remember.

And if he tried to stay curled up inside his little cave of a mind too long, sooner or later THE WORD would come along to pry him out.

And PAIN would follow.

So setting his doubts aside, he gloried in this wonder of movement.

And though the larger pattern he sought still eluded him, the dance gradually wound through the darkness to a place wholly new.

A place of light.

Not in his surroundings. They remained dark and dimensionless and devoid of meaning.

And not quite in his mind, either. That was a place he was by now well acquainted with, though resembling nothing so much as a barren jail cell.

More in his....

Memory?

He saw — or he dreamed — a sun. Glowing and pulsing beneath him. He knew he hadn't long to live. That was of no importance.

Because he also had forever.

The clear white light.

He discarded his body layer by layer, replacing it with the pure energy of the sun. His eyes were already gone. What need had he of eyes, when all the glory of the universe stood revealed before him? Infusing him with a fullness beyond human comprehension.

And yet a single strand of existence still held him to the world and human desires. A wonder to rival all that lay revealed before him.

He searched for its source.

And found her there in the center of his mind. Staring in wonder at this transformation overtaking him. Reaching for him.

As he was reaching back. Reaching from this palace of sunlight where all was complete, all was certain, all was right because all the universe existed in one single moment of time, churning out variations that in the end were all just different faces of the One.

He did not want to leave such luxuriant certainty. And yet love drew his fingers forth. Toward her. Reaching for her face as his mind called her name.

ARVADA!

PAIN.

***

"Arvada, please! I beg you."

"You're always begging. Just one thing after another. I told you, we're still fighting here. I can't spare the troops."

"Just a squad. Home in on their transmission and force the damn doors open. Blast them if you have to. Just—"

"There's too many Grinders between here and interface."

"But—" Didn't she understand? His mother and Elva were....

Were what?

Drowning! Drowning, yes. In the ... in the next corridor. Somehow Sahan had gotten separated from them. In the dark. In Interface. Now all the openings were sealed and locked, and he couldn't reach them, and water from ruptured pipes was pouring in. They'd called him, desperate, letting him know they were inches away from drowning.

He should never have left them. Only ... only something intervened. Not important now.

"Arvada, the Grinders set an auto-destruct device. A series of rockets to destabilize the torus ring. I disabled it for you, or the torus would be breaking itself to pieces against the radiation shielding right now."

"You?" She laughed. Laughed! "Disabled rockets mounted on the ring? How?"

"I...." Yes, how? He had some vague memory of red lozenges spinning in his mind. Of clamping down on them somehow, and of pain.

"Arvada, please! You can't just let them die!"

"Sorry, Sahan. I have Grinders to fight. Sattar out."

The transmission went dead. He braced himself to try again, but saw that he had no radio, nor helmet. He forgot how he'd been talking to her.

But now he could hear his mother and Elva, calling to him.

"Sahan! Sahan! Help us!"

Right on the other side of this wall. An array of pipes ran along it. He began grabbing them and ripping them loose from their mountings. As sections of the wall came exposed, he beat on them with the bottoms of his fists. He had to open a breach, let out the water from the opposite corridor.

"Sahan!" It was Elva. Her voice was weak. And terrified. "Quickly! The water keeps rising. Your mother—" Her voice choked off.

"No!" he screamed. He tried kicking the wall, with no better success.

"Sahan ... Sa—"

There came a brief gurgling sound, then silence.

Sahan sank to his knees. A giant fist squeezed his insides.

No. No. His mother. Elva. It couldn't be. They'd loved him. And he'd let them die. Too busy battling the auto-destruct in order to give Captain Sattar one more glorious victory. No more than a stepping-stool to her. Like always.

And now he'd killed the only two people in the world who truly cared for him. They'd counted on him, and even as the water rose around them he turned away to serve—

In one word he screamed out his pain:

ARVADA!

Chapter 11

It took several hours to fight their way through the sections of the ship the Evolved had blown up.

By that time all six combat groups had to send the Riggers forward to spell the Marines. Aside from taking horrendous casualties, the blue suits were wholly exhausted from the strain of crawling through the fractured, debris-choked, dust-laden wreckage, constantly expecting a Grinder to spring from ambush right in their face. And too often finding their expectations met.

Arvada had been concerned over how the Riggers would handle this kind of butchery. Most of them had never been in combat before. Captain LeFleur, the Marine who'd supervised most of their training, assured her they'd do just fine.

"They've all been chased from their homes," he'd told her. "The way they see it, the way back is paved with Grinder corpses. Besides, they don't have enough experience to know just how bad it really is."

And so it proved. The Riggers tore into the Grinders with a fury. It helped that by this time the Grinders' numbers were severely diminished. Even in the tight quarters, an attacked Rigger's winger could generally squeeze forward in time to aid a comrade.

It helped too, though Arvada never mentioned it and quickly shushed any who did, that a primitive fury even beyond the battle norm appeared to be spreading among the Peregrines. Marines and Riggers alike. She herself had observed it in the Grinders, who early in the battle for the blown-up sections appeared to have abandoned cunning for rank ferocity.

It had worked for a while. The Marine advance repeatedly came to a halt as even these superbly trained soldiers, many with combat experience under her or Sahan, got rattled and froze in place, anticipating attack from any direction in the cramped bubbles enclosing them.

Then whatever was churning the Grinders into animalistic fury began to seep into the Peregrine fighters as well.

Having experienced these waves of emotion herself, and exercised the resultant savagery on a Grinder springing on her from above, Arvada had her own ideas. She believed the intensity of the combat was supercharging the animal implants serving as the neural bed for the Peregrines' enhanced perceptions. Which included, among other species, bats and dolphins for echo location and radar, snakes for infrared, sharks for magnetic and electric fields, pheromones, and pressure waves; and cats for engaging the maximum amount of neural circuitry in the mammalian attention reflex.

Predators all.

The Grinders too must have implants. Though at this point in the war no Grinder body had been recovered with their brains intact. From observation in battle it appeared that the Grinders' senses functioned over a somewhat more narrow range. But their implants and the Peregrines' came from the same original source — the Riggers of the *Stephen Hawking*.

Were these berserker impulses something she should worry about? Probably. But she didn't see anything she could do about it. And victory was too close. She could smell it. With her shark receptors? Arvada grinned at what may or may not have been a joke.

Moving forward behind the Riggers' advance, she established a temporary command post in a small pocket in the rubble a short way to the rear. With no light she saw the whole scene in shades of green from her radar, rendered slightly blurry from the dust in the air. Pieces of broken beams and piping and curtains of sundered wiring drooped from the shattered roof. A pair of legs in silver-green armor projected from the debris pile that formed the left wall. Just in case the Grinder wasn't as dead as it looked — she couldn't see the head — Arvada cut one of its legs off with her battle-saw. The blood emerged a heated red rapidly cooling toward rust as it soaked into the dust-covered floor.

"So what happens when we break through?" asked Keir Gephardt, XO of the *Usagi*.

"Break through to what?" asked someone.

"To the Evolved," Arvada declared. So she hoped, anyway. The possibility existed that this ship was being run entirely by its holobrain. That would be a great disappointment. She wanted to get her hands on something alive.

Taking out another Evolved heavy would get more of Catalan's fleet over to thinking the future lay with the Alliance. It would leave the Evolved with only three heavies in the entire Peregrine System, making the Grinder-occupied habitats in the outlying systems more vulnerable.

And it would further intimidate the living Evolved, already reeling from Sahan's destruction of the Master Holobrain aboard the *Elipida*.

Sahan. A sudden ache pried open her heart.

Think of victory. Think of revenge.

She wanted an Evolved alive, dammit. *That* would seriously demoralize the others. That would make them think long and hard about just how superior they were, and how much this war really meant to them.

"We need to find the Evolved in charge of this ship," she said. "There may only be one, but we need him."

"What if now that the Grinders are dealt with, they blow up the entire ship?" asked Jamaya Torhena of the *Cressida*. Tense murmurs underscored her question.

What if? Six cruisers, every one loaded to the gills with infantry. The Riggers would be difficult to replace from a diminishing pool, the painstakingly trained Marines impossible. Regular civilians couldn't fight; few had the complete array of sensors, and fewer still had ever learned to use them in suits.

"They won't," she stated.

"How can you be so sure?" questioned Jamaya.

"Because like I keep telling you, the Evolved will be too afraid to die."

Nobody sounded reassured, though their belly-aching diminished to mumbles. They all knew something about Sahan Kotori, including his supposed penetration of the holobrains. But none truly understood, and not all believed, even now.

Like Jamaya. "You told us, but how afraid can they be? They're soldiers, like us."

"Commander Torhena, you are in no way qualified to question my orders in this matter. My knowledge comes from sources and experience outside your own. And even if you were, does this really strike you as the proper time? Now carry out the task you've been assigned."

"No one's questioning your authority, Captain Sattar," said Keir Gephart, though Jamaya Torhena had stepped at least one foot across that line, nor was Arvada likely to forget it. "But presuming there are Evolved on board, how do we find them?"

"They will come to us," Arvada declared.

If they truly were here. If not, if this whole ship was being run by the holobrain, possibly as a decoy while the last three made a run from Harrar's Reach. And then Jamaya's fear about the Evolved blowing up the ship veered toward extremely likely.

Well, since you couldn't play it both ways, she'd just have to settle on this one.

"Once we find the holobrain," she said, "we need to gather all the intelligence we can. There are several sections that Intel has identified as possible sites for a command and control center. I will make for one of them with my group. Captain Gephart, I believe you already have coordinates for the other."

"Acknowledged."

"Is there any chance at all," asked Captain Severin of the *Mista*, "that we could pilot this ship back to our own territory?"

Tempting. So-o-o tempting.

"Regrettably, no," Arvada replied. "That would be ideal, but it would involve making a Jump while relying on systems and technology we haven't time to master. It would be all too easy for the Evolved to set up a decoy system that might do anything, including deliver the ship back to Harrar's Reach under the guns of their other heavies."

"Do you think there could be more Grinders in reserve?" asked Gephart.

"I think it unlikely. Why deliberately lose a battle piecemeal? But of course you will all stay alert. If you find something of intelligence value, don't linger longer than it takes to make the best record of it you can. We're looking for the big picture here.

"Aside from the bridge, or possibly bridges," she continued, "we most want to find the magazines. Because if by the time we finish conducting our basic recon the Evolved still haven't come forward and surrendered, we will rig the magazines to explode and be on our way. Let's get to it, people."

Leaving the channel active, she hurriedly checked to make sure all her equipment was in place. More, in fact, like patting herself over to make sure she was real.

People talked about butterflies in the stomach.

She had eagles.

CAPTAIN SATTAR, came a voice that seemed to originate in the center of her head. THE AUTO-DESTRUCT SEQUENCE HAS BEEN INITIATED. YOU AND YOUR PEOPLE HAVE FIFTEEN MINUTES TO LEAVE THIS SHIP.

Chapter 12

THE MOVEMENTS OF THE dance were beginning to extend deeper into his body.

It was a strange sensation, independent of any link to either gravity or breath. Memories came back to him, of shifting balance, of sinking his weight wholly through one ... foot, of *rooting* himself to the ground. And something, dimmer and more abstract, beyond; of pulling opponents forward as he sank, spinning them off their feet, hurling them far away.

He had after all been human, then. Probably. The memories, fragmentary as they were, could be implanted in a created brain. But for now he would assume he had been a *people*. And some sort of fighter as well. Yes, that stirred up other memories, though he couldn't follow them out.

All the more frustrating, then, that even as he tried to replicate such movements he could not actually sink his weight into the ground. He couldn't find any ground. Couldn't find anything but darkness beyond his rather cloudy perception of his own boundaries.

Instead what happened when memories of grounding came to him, a vague sense of materialization originated within what was becoming defined as his leg, then rippled downward. Eventually dissipating not into any ground, but rather into darkness and a few scraps of half-remembered sensation.

It would undoubtedly help if up and down would fix themselves in place. They tended to be fairly stable, but sometimes everything rotated.

Another remembered sensation persistently eluded him. One closer to his center. Center, that is, as defined as that cavity connecting his arms and legs, where he had no sensory record at all. Memory suggested that there should be a lot of activity taking place there. Breathing, heartbeat, digestion, all sorts.

Only not for him.

He exerted all his will to direct his concentration toward this area. Hoping for it to burst into sudden activity like an engine stuttering into life after long idleness.

It didn't.

Yet oh so slowly something, something ... the *dan tien*, that was it! Vishnu but he was brilliant — took form low in his belly. "Low" defined as closer to his legs than his arms.

Dammit, he needed to breathe! Not to fend off the sensation of smothering — he'd learned to ignore that reflex long ago — but to locate and give force to this *dan tien* he'd so newly discovered. *That* would give life to his movements! Breath and breath alone. To swell, to compress, to feel the whole body shifting around that ball of livid energy, this was....

Tai Chi!

Yes, yes. The dance he'd been doing, it had a name. And a purpose, vaster than any dance. A destination, pointing toward the infinite.

The Tai Chi could free him, if only he could let its pulsating energy fill his body and lead him where his true fate wished him to go.

But he needed *breath!*

He needed—

Something smashed into him. Something hard and fast and hurtling from a universe he thought contained only him. The impact sent him tumbling around and around, locked with his assailant.

Terror swept over him. Though he hadn't heard THE WORD, fear clenched him tight. But the heightened sense of physicality the Tai Chi had wrought in him also furnished new sensations for the fear to exploit. Fangs struck deep inside him, spewing out caustic poison. The colored lines outlining his body vibrated at blurring frequency, shattering any attempt at self-control.

Riding the terror came a blast of hate. Hate sharp as a sword pointed at his throat.

There was another creature in here with him!

Open hands struck his throat. Then squeezed down.

He was strangling.

But how, when he couldn't even breathe? Yet his body still sucked desperately for air. His head, previously so amorphous, became etched clearly in pain as it swelled to bursting.

He could not die like this! He'd put in too much effort, endured too much pain. Had too many questions still unanswered.

He possessed *life!* Human or artificial no longer mattered. He lived.

And that life had a purpose. A sacred quest suddenly revealed to him.

ARVADA!

He flinched reflexively in anticipation of the PAIN. But it did not come.

Could it not find him here?

The creature, this demon at his neck, lusted for his life with a hatred born of darkness and terror and an all-embracing isolation.

But his own hatred sprang from roots fully as deep.

And this Other's hate emanated from the realm of death. While he, Sahan Kotori — him, him, him, unmistakably *him* ¬— still lived.

Death had tried so often to defeat him. Yet here he stood.

ARVADA!

The attacker's hands still dug into his neck. But Sahan's own hands, which had felt so vague, so feeble a moment before, now became infused with the power of hatred burning bright with the strength of life.

He pulled his attacker's hands loose. He still could not breathe, but he was no longer strangling. The Hate, and the Terror that brought it, began to dissipate within his grasp.

He came back to the familiar darkness, unthreatened.

With strange memories. Of....

Arvada.

PAIN.

Chapter 13

OH MY GOD, SHE thought, as the God-like voice still rang not in her ears, but between them. Was that what — who — I thought it was? Telling me I had fifteen minutes to scurry back to the *Geirovar* with my tail between my legs?

Arvada suppressed an urge to laugh. The other commanders would not find the situation so funny. She brushed off some of the dust fallen from the wrecked roof, as though it was the force of the voice that had shaken it loose.

She'd heard a voice just like it once before. Only then it was demanding that she surrender her ship. A lot of good people died that day. And Sahan lost part of his mind sending the Evolved to a very literal hell.

"CAPTAIN SATTAR. THIS IS YOUR LAST WARNING. EVACUATE YOUR PEOPLE OR FACE DESTRUCTION."

In her earphones she heard the other five group commanders muttering to each other about what they'd just heard. Such poor discipline reflected badly on her. Oh well, when you were a twenty-eight year old Lieutenant Commander leading the whole Peregrine fleet on no authority but your reputation, you couldn't expect the same snap-to-attention obedience as if sanctioned by "legitimate authority." She'd slap them into line yet.

"I appreciate the warning," she said to the broken walls with their protruding sections of shattered pipe and draped wires, some still live and sparking. Her voice was not quite as steady as she would like, but what the hell.

"Only with respect," she added, "you are full of shit."

The concerned mutterings from the other commanders rose sharply in intensity.

"Cut the chatter, people," she snapped. And to the Evolved: "Go ahead and pound your chest all you want. I know you don't want to die. In fact I know exactly how *badly* you don't want to die. I learned from Sahan Kotori. Recognize the name? The man who infiltrated the holobrain of a ship just like this one and sent its commander, another of you self-proclaimed 'Evolved,' straight into the Terror Barrier? And yes, I do know what that means. Sahan gave me quite a graphic description. I also know that with the Master Holobrain at Harrar's Reach destroyed, you'll suffer the same fate. Sounds pretty gloomy to me."

She paused to allow him to beat his chest. Nothing. "Now it may be that you're brave beyond imagining, and an eternity quivering in terror strikes you as a perfectly reasonable price to pay for a bunch of dead Peregrines. If so, go ahead and blow the ship."

YOUR INFORMATION IS FALSE. I STAND IN NO SUCH PERIL.

"You mean Sahan Kotori just made it up off the top of his head? And I suppose the Evolved who rode his ship down into the Sun died of old age, or maybe a stubbed toe. In that case, you'll have a lot of company when you die. But only for a little while. Because that's the other thing about the Terror Barrier, isn't it? You're all alone. For ever and ever."

Thinking of Sahan really made her want to get her hands on this posturer. To twist parts off of him just to wave the bloody roots in his face.

YOUR MISCONCEPTIONS WILL COST YOUR PEOPLE DEAR.

Steady. You have a job to do.

"You see, this is something I don't understand. You know Sahan killed one of you, right within his ship's own holobrain. Yet you can't seem to grasp the simple fact that Sahan was smarter and stronger than you. And I loved him." There. It felt so good to say it openly, after all these years. She didn't care what the other commanders thought of it.

YOUR EMOTIONS ARE OF NO RELEVANCE TO ME.

"Now I'm thinking maybe Sahan understood the Terror Barrier better than you do. After all, he went there. And came out again. Nothing any Evolved has ever done. If you really don't know that without the Master Holobrain you cannot be assimilated into the Group Mind, and will instead face an eternity of horror, then man, are you in for a shock. Meanwhile, the clock's down to eleven minutes. You notice we are not withdrawing to our ships."

THEN DIE.

"Group leaders, converge on the source of the transmissions."

Yeah she was scared. And not half so confident as she sounded. It was a hell of a responsibility, risking the crews of six ships.

At the same time, she was thrilled to the gills. This was how you became Arvada Sattar.

"If I were you," she told the Evolved, "I'd start thinking long and hard about where I want to spend eternity. Then start discussing terms."

YOU DOOM YOUR PEOPLE OVER YOUR OWN PRIDE. FOR WHICH YOU ARE WELL KNOWN.

"Unconditional surrender, would be a good place to start."

Chapter 14

She expected something exotic.

After all, Arvada had never seen a living Evolved. Maybe the traitor Raisa Catalan and some of her henchmen had. But no one in the Resistance. The Evolved kept to their ships. Even in the occupied habitats they exercised their rule through the Grinders, who were in turn controlled by the on-site holobrain.

Naturally expectations built up.

Seven feet tall maybe, built like Adonis, with a palpable aura of … something. Wavering lights in the warm tones. Mystical power. The sort of spiritual/physical bond Sahan had developed to such a pitch, only magnified and made somehow visual. Strong enough to leap tall buildings in a single bound, yet so delicate of touch a sparrow could not take wing from their open hand because their yielding energy was so fine the bird could find nothing to push against. Oh, and telepathy, of course. Maybe even a touch of spoon-bending — telekinesis, that was it.

What she got was a male human who, properly attired, could walk from one end of the *Geirovar* to the other without attracting attention.

Well-built, true, but no more than the Marines or other Peregrines who stayed active. Handsome enough, in a slim, painstakingly ascetic fashion Arvada found off-putting for its irreversible hint of disdain. But certainly possessed of no other-worldly beauty. He moved well, but again with no more grace than her or others who made serious study of the internal arts.

And if he had paranormal abilities, she'd just have to learn about them the hard way.

What did stand out, however, was that he wore no pigtail like the Riggers and Marines. No direct, wired connection from suit to brain. Whatever data and whatever messages he received, and according to Sahan both the density and depth considerably exceeded those of the Peregrines, came straight from the holobrain.

Arvada had also nursed visions of meeting her first Evolved in exotic quarters, all shifting lights and gauzy globules and flowing, ephemeral curtains of unknown material exhausting every shade of purple known to man and a few that pushed beyond the boundaries of normal perception.

But if the Evolved's private quarters really did possess some futuristic Arabian Knights quality, she was never to know.

Because as she led her party, locked and loaded, toward the bridge, he came down the corridors to meet her. Dressed in sky blue top and bottom disappointingly close to the Alliance Navy's fatigues, but for the color.

"Captain Sattar," he told her, coming forward with his hands in plain sight but no gesture of respect, fellowship, or surrender. "I suggest you hasten to remove your boarding parties. The auto-destruct is now truly engaged. I trust twenty minutes will suffice? To get your cruisers clear as well? There is now no way I can stop the device. Let us therefore hasten."

This time she did not dare call his bluff. There might still be other Evolved aboard; the auto-destruct might be a hoax, and as soon as her cruisers drew off the ship would attempt another Jump.

At least the enemy wouldn't be firing on her ships as they sped off. Not unless they wanted to kill her prisoner. From what Sahan had told her, they would never condemn one of their own to the Terror Barrier.

And so they all scrambled back to the cruisers. They fought a desultory rear-guard action against the Grinders, but not enough of the enemy remained to seriously impede the withdrawal. The wounded had already been evacuated, thank God. They managed to get out most of their dead as well.

A few bodies remained lost amid the blood-soaked wreckage. Several of the Captains made a *pro forma* request to lead parties, for which there were plentiful volunteers, to recover the lost bodies. It was an old tradition, but Arvada denied permission. She was not about to lose valuable crew just to fill the freezers with dead and dismembered flesh.

Nor could she let it be anything more to her.

***

As for Arvada's dreams of parlaying with the Evolved amid splendiferous and futuristic surroundings, after they'd both gone through basic decontamination she conducted her initial interview in her own cabin aboard the *Geirovar*. Arvada could tell from the Evolved's sneer he was unimpressed.

They sat at her table over coffee, which he rather surprised her by accepting. She sniffed in the warm aroma hungrily. Normally the ship's coffee followed the centuries-old tradition of strong and indifferent, but now the scent helped dispel the stench of blood she found difficult to clear from her nostrils. The bitterness of the brew also sluiced out the suggestions of dust clinging to her throat, though her suit filters had kept her from actually breathing it.

The Evolved drank his coffee without reaction, negative or positive. Of course he had not had to sully his nostrils, let alone his hands, killing Grinders in the wreckage.

Normally Arvada sat with her back to the *faux* space window. This time she indicated for her captive, which was what he damn well was despite his airs, to take that seat. Having dismissed her guard, she did not want to be pinned in place should the situation turn violent.

Which she did not expect, but adhering to rote precautions was easier than guessing whether or not they were needed and improvising some last-second response if you were wrong. She was confident enough about her abilities against most men —Sahan excepted; but Sahan was a special case and god*damn* she missed him — but the Evolved was still an unknown.

"You have a name?" she asked by way of opening.

"Call me Beck," he replied after a moment's hesitation.

"Beck." She mulled that one over. "There was a Beck Egan, long ago. A Rigger, and a hero of the revolution against Earth."

"Names of the Founders are not uncommon among us."

His voice, like so much else about him, was disappointingly ordinary. Deep and resonant; he might have distinguished himself as an actor or singer. But still pedestrianly *human*. Nothing of that omnipotent between-the-ears sensation she'd received aboard his ship. Undoubtedly a mechanical ploy exercised through her own suit's audio sensors.

But it would not do to underestimate him. Could he read her mind, maybe? Even manipulate it? Arvada examined her mental state for any waves or tickles or unusual urges or whatever signs such powers would cause. Nothing. The information she'd picked up from Sahan indicated a holobrain would be necessary for any mental manipulations. But how would she know?

She found herself rather wishing he did possess such a skill. She'd gone and captured an Evolved, dammit, something no one else had ever done. A member of the race who'd smashed the combined Earth and Peregrine fleets at Demeter and pretty much run wild ever since. Now she had him, and she wanted at least a hint of something marvelous to distinguish her trophy.

"Captain!" came an urgent call from the bridge.

One of walls, which she'd dialed down to a pastel purple-gray, switched to the bridge screens. It showed the Evolved ship sitting in space. Looking uncomfortably close; her fleet had already put a lot of distance between them but the monitors scaled it to constant size.

Suddenly the ship vanished in a flash of yellow and white. Bits of wreckage could be seen flying into space. The light quickly faded, leaving a few large and twisted sheets of metal reflecting the glow of the sun. Another screen opened on the opposite wall, showing both colored fields and numbers analyzing the spreading field now slowly sinking toward the sun. Arvada summed it up quickly; space garbage floating through a field of high radioactivity and chemical compounds, dissipating before her eyes.

Scratch one holobrain.

Beck said nothing, looking on the screens with no expression.

"So you lost your ship," she said without the least hint of pity. "That makes two I've destroyed. With one Evolved in the Terror Barrier and one captive. War's not so easy an enterprise as you thought, is it?"

"*You* took *one*," he stated. His blue eyes narrowed; amazing how much hatred he could express with no other facial manipulation at all. "Your servitor, the madman Sahan Kotori, took the other."

"Fair enough," she acknowledged, storing away the insult to Sahan for later consideration. "But I took yours."

"Illegally."

"Illegally? You invade our system unprovoked, destroy our habitats, kill our citizens, then whine to me about legalities?"

"Peace talks are still being conducted at the *Kepler* between the legitimate Peregrine government, headed by Raisa Catalan—"

"Bullshit."

"— and the rebel Citizens' Council. A truce has been declared. Your action here is in flagrant violation of that truce."

She sipped her coffee, put the cup down delicately, inhaling one last soothing cloud of the stimulatingly bitter steam.

"Truce? Your first demand was that the Peregrine fleet dock at the *Kepler*, and discharge all their crews. While your ships, and the traitor Catalan's, flew around free as a bird. That's not a truce, that's bend-over-and-take-it-up-the-ass surrender. Fortunately many of the Alliance ships didn't fall for it. They ignored the Council's directive and came to me instead. As for those Alliance ships that did dock according to this 'truce'" — she paused for a deep breath, sick with the stupidity and cowardice of her own people — "you destroyed them where they lay. I guess that's what you call legal, huh?"

"That only took place *after* your barbaric attack on Harrar's Reach. And, I would note, it did not involve killing any of their crews. It was *you* — Arvada Sattar, and your puppet-demon Sahan Kotori—"

Rising half out of her chair, Arvada lunged across the table and slapped him. Beck's arm started to rise to block the blow; she could see he was quick enough, but he held short and accepted it. His head swung to the side, then he settled back into place unmoved.

"That," he said, "is a violation of the rules of war. But I suppose from someone who slaughters innocent civilians *en masse* I should consider it no more than a mild rebuke.

"If you want to call Sahan a demon," she returned levelly, "feel free. To your people, he was. And I'm proud of that. There's not one thing he ever did in this war I am not proud of. But do *not* call him a puppet. Not mine, or anyone else's."

A look of amusement crept into his steel blue eyes. "No? We shall see."

"What does that mean?" Arvada asked uneasily.

"But as I was saying before you assaulted me, it was you who first violated the truce."

"A truce I never accepted."

"Killing over three thousand of your own people in the process. Civilians. For which you have been declared a war criminal. Not just by the *legitimate* Peregrine government of Admiral Catalan, but both your own Naval Command and Citizens' Council as well. Did you not know? You have been ordered to report to the *Kepler* and submit yourself for trial."

Take a deep breath. Into the *dan tien*, so he doesn't see it.

"Okay, so I'm a war criminal." She spread her palms in a so-what gesture. "I suppose they're giving good-conduct medals to those Captains who obeyed the Council's orders, and are now staring at the wreckage of their ships."

Her bravado was forced. Arvada hadn't known she'd been declared a war criminal. By her own Citizens' Council, no less. No ships from the Kepler system had come to her since Sahan's attack on Harrar's Reach, and she was well beyond range of electromagnetic communication.

She'd known the destruction of the *Elipida* would be condemned. But three thousand deaths? Arvada had a hard time swallowing that herself. Even though the dead, while technically civilians, had worked providing logistics and intelligence for the Evolved. She'd hoped the toll would be much lower.

At first she'd rejected Sahan's proposal. Not just over the prospect of civilian casualties, but because of the virtual certainty that he'd be killed.

But then the Citizen's Council did its best to hand over the Alliance fleet to the Evolved. Basically duplicating Catalan's actions early in the war.

At that point the war was lost. Unless they could find some way to shock the Evolved into re-thinking the whole enterprise.

Like destroying the Master Holobrain at Harrar's Reach.

Impossible. Just impossible.

For anyone but *maybe* Sahan.

So okay, they'd killed a bunch of civilians. Quote-unquote civilians.

It was still an awful lot of them.

The ships following Arvada wouldn't know about the Council's declaration. Not yet. But soon they must. And then?

Then some would continue to follow her, and others wouldn't. And what of Earth? They'd rather tentatively been sending her ships in an effort to delay the Evolved from attacking them. Would Earth keep sending aid to someone whose own government declared a war criminal?

Arvada had set the Evolved back on their heels. But without immediate and sustained follow-up, they would recover. Reinforcements could presumably be sent. Maybe even another Master Holobrain.

Without her, the Resistance would lack any coherent response. An element of vanity weighed in that appraisal, true. But Arvada was the one single *battle leader* the Alliance could point to. She'd fought time and again. And won.

Damn! She'd known Catalan's government would condemn her. But the Citizens' Council?

It was outrageous. It was absurd. It was *wrong*.

Sort of.

It was also a problem.

Beck's naturally arrogant expression was deepened by a smirk. "Should you reject the Citizens' Council's authority, you and those who follow you will be no better than bandits."

"Just so long as we're victorious bandits. And it looks like we're off to a pretty good start, doesn't it?"

That caused a flicker of irritation to bend down the upraised corner of his lips. "Will Earth see it that way? And how many of those commanders senior in rank to you will continue to follow your orders when to do so means branding themselves criminals as well? They only defer to you now because...."

In a disconcertingly human gesture he waved his hands, searching for a suitably devastating phrase. "Because it's become something of a rebel fashion, as far as I can see."

"Maybe. But two dead Evolved heavies make a hell of a fashion statement."

"Let us stop this bantering. Having captured me, it is now your clear duty to take me to the *Kepler* and present me to your Citizens' Council as a prisoner of war. Even though taken during a state of truce."

"Thank you for making my duty clear. I would strongly suggest you don't make a habit of it. As for the Council, I will deal with them in my own good time. I'm a war criminal, remember?"

"If you refuse, it is no more than an open acknowledge of your guilt. That you and all who follow you are outlaws, to be shunned by all bodies who govern according to rules of law. That you are outside the bounds of civilization."

Easy, easy. You're in charge here, not him. Don't let your temper reverse that.

"By 'civilized' I take it you mean one that invades a peaceful people without provocation?"

"I warn you—"

She hurled her coffee at him. It came too fast for her to stop. He uttered a cry of pain and surprise. Trying to wipe the hot liquid from his face, he slid toward the side of the desk to get on his feet. He was quick, but so was Arvada. She got there before him. She did not call for Security.

He stared at her, quivering with indecision. Fury slowly turned toward petulance. He slid back into place. She resumed her chair.

"That is the second time you have assaulted me," he muttered.

"That is also the second time you have tried to tell me my duty. If I'd kill three thousand of my own people, just imagine what I might do to you."

Eyes flaring, he started to speak, then cut it off with a grunt.

"Is that another warning I see in your eyes?" she asked. "Perhaps a 'you wouldn't dare'? Wouldn't dare what, do you suppose? Put you out an airlock? In all truth, probably not. Not after I went to all this trouble capturing you. Wouldn't dare beat you silly? Even if it takes a couple of Security people to help me? Only one way to find out. Why don't you dare me, and see what happens?"

Smoldering, he leaned back against the wall, that displayed a wide and enhanced, though still mostly empty, expanse of space behind him. Which despite her disavowal, was just where she longed to put him.

Reset, woman. Stop thinking with your spleen.

"Are you hungry?" she asked. She herself was ravenous. Battle and sex both affected her that way.

He did not answer.

Something sweet and decadent. Light and fluffy and as far from thoughts of killing Grinders as you could get. And to demonstrate to this would-be Superman just what a pampered member of an inferior race had reduced his ship to space dust.

She pressed "Send" on the console before her. "Two donuts. One glazed, one chocolate."

Those would come from the dispensers. Made by robots, which always lent such dainties an impersonal quality and whose unvarying mediocrity bred a lack of anticipation over the years. But life at sea had always been hard. Drake and Magellan's men probably complained about their donuts too.

"So are you going to take me to your Citizens' Council or not?" he asked. Surly. No sweet tooth, these Evolved.

"Why would I do that?"

"We've discussed this. I am a prisoner of war, and they are the closest approach to legitimate authority available to your insurrection."

Insurrection, no less. "Yes, you're a prisoner of war. My war, my prisoner. If the Council wants one, let them and Naval Command go get an Evolved of their own."

He leaned forward over his elbows, lips tightening.

"I make no threats and issue no warnings," he said. "But you are a barbarian."

"Fine. I'm barbarian. Since we're bandying words about, what would you call those who rigged the torus *Enodia* to beat itself to pieces against its radiation shield? Or those who set up rockets to cause the *Eustella* to tear itself to pieces, only Sahan again entered the holobrain and defeated your device? What would you call the people who created the Grinders? Oh right, I forgot. *Civilized*."

"You cannot possibly know what we are. It is beyond your mind's conceiving."

Well, what had she expected? Arvada pressed a button on her console. The doors to her cabin parted and in walked two Security members, specially trained Marines. Two more stood outside. They wore partial armor and carried pistols, batons, and various non-lethal devices. Their movements were measured, suggestive of a crouch. Their eyes were cautious, but hard.

"Escort our guest to his new quarters."

"Quarters, Captain?" asked the Sergeant.

"Yes," Arvada told her. "In the brig. I want him under eyeball surveillance 24/7, with two security officers present at all times. If he presents a risk you judge serious, you are authorized to use deadly force."

"Captain."

Once more Beck started to his feet in anger, only to find himself hemmed in. Seeing the Sergeant's hand go to the club on her hip, he settled back.

"You would treat me like a common criminal?" he asked, surprisingly calm.

"A little worse, actually. And should you make any attempt at obstruction, you will find yourself in restraints."

She heard his teeth grind. So human!

"Did you ever read *Gulliver's Travels*, Captain?"

"No. Have you?"

"Not in its entirety. I encountered it in a survey of Earth literature. There is a scene in which the hero is bound to the ground by, ah, Lilliputians, I believe they're called. Were the holobrain still functioning I could tell you exactly, but no matter. They are a tiny people, less than a tenth of his size. Yet they hold him fast. I understand his position now."

Arvada swiveled around as he was ushered from her cabin.

"You've had a lot of your horizons expanded today, haven't you? Literary and otherwise."

Chapter 15

HE WALKED FAST THROUGH the corridors, sometimes stumbling. He had to get to his quarters. His XO's quarters aboard the ... the *Mettalise*? *Viveca*? He couldn't remember.

Whatever, he had to get there before anyone saw him like this. Muttering and moaning and smashing his fist against the walls. Reeling from side to side, banging into the walls, which had grown closer together than he remembered.

But he kept going in circles. He knew his quarters should be just ahead. But they never were.

Was he even First Officer anymore? Or had Arvada given that away to that wretched Earther Duncan Mallory too? She'd given him everything else. Including herself.

I'll kill him!

But first he had to shut himself from view.

He put his hands over his ears. She was *fucking* him! Right now, he could hear it. What, were they piping it over the whole ship? Was the video playing on the bridge screens? Was everyone aboard cheering along? Was this how she ran her ship ever since....

Ever since what?

Since she stuffed him in the cockpit of the hunter-killer, forcing him to take Mallory's place in that suicide mission against Harrar's Reach.

ARVADA!

A cry or rage, or despair? Had he shouted aloud? He bit down on his lip to keep from doing it again. Blood trickled down his throat. Bitter and metallic. Like her heart.

Wait. Hadn't he died at Harrar's Reach? He was sure. Then how could he....

Where *was* he? *When* was he? And where was his Kali-plagued room?

Speakers lining the corridor blared out her laughter, her moans as she and Mallory crawled all over each other. The hot, moist sounds pierced through the hands clutched over his ears. He could *feel* her skin, as if Mallory's hands had become his own.

Why hadn't he died? How close could you come, yet be brought back only to be hurled against the pain once more?

Would she never let him go?

ARVADA!

She stood before him.

A sudden appearance. A fulcrum to lever the agony in him to fresh intensity.

He saw her loam-colored hair spectrum-streaked by glowing sunlight, though the corridor itself showed dull and gray.

The sun! Give me back the sun! The sun where I died.

He stumbled forward a few steps, hands held out before him.

"Arvada, please. What is going on? I don't understand any of this."

"My God, you've come back," she said wonderingly. "My own personal zombie. Why can't you just stay dead? I showed you the way. Don't come begging to me now." Her voice bit into him like radiation from the sun at Harrar's Reach knocking his atoms loose from one another. "It's your own self-pity dragged you here, not me."

"Then kill me! Please, just let me die. Stop *hurting* me!"

"Why should I go to the trouble? Let your death be on your own head. Self-inflicted wounds, Sahan. That's the whole story of your life." She shook her head disgustedly. "And now look. Is this what you had to do in order to come crawling back? Go on. *Look.*"

What was she talking about? Sahan looked down.

And staggered back. Had the air been evacuated from the corridor? Vacuum sucked his heart, his guts, the breath in his nostrils right out of him.

He'd become a Grinder.

He wore no fighting suit. His naked flesh stood out raw as though in pulling loose, the suit had stripped his skin away with it, leaving each separate muscle fiber and viscera exposed. His body was thin, his arms almost skeletal, but dense with muscles twitching and sliding against each other, a nauseating shifting of green and yellow.

But ... he wasn't a Grinder! Had never been a Grinder. Illusion, all some cruel illusion.

Only from the repellant frown with which Arvada surveyed him he knew she saw the same abomination.

He wanted to explain that this wasn't really him. Only he had no explanation. He took a step forward, meaning to beg her to tell him how this had happened.

Duncan Mallory stood between them.

"Back! Back!" He made threatening feints with the battle-saw held out in front of him, as though Sahan were some animal to be cowed.

Arvada laughed.

"This isn't *me!*" Sahan shouted. Or tried to. But he talked around a mouthful of stones, unable even to understand himself.

He shot his hand to his mouth. Something held it away from his face. Then he realized. Teeth. Grinder teeth. Blocky and protuberant and distorting his mouth beyond his lips' ability to form coherent syllables.

Still Mallory advanced on him. Pushing him back further and further from Arvada. Treating him like the beast she undoubtedly thought him. Making a spectacle of him.

I'll kill him.

Could he get around the prodding saw? Dangerous, but if he could sideslip and parry the saw behind the blade, he could move in and rip Mallory's throat out with his teeth. Show Arvada her lover paddling in his own blood.

His teeth? But he was *not* a Grinder.

Was he human, then?

What *was* he?

The whirring blade jabbed within inches of his face. Mallory laughed. Arvada laughed.

He couldn't fight. Not Mallory, not Arvada, not anyone. There was just no spirit left in him.

He wanted to plead with Arvada. For something; he knew not what. Just to help him make it all end. Dreams, life, the pain, all of it.

She watched him with withering disgust.

Sahan turned and broke into a shambling jog down the corridor. If nothing else, let him hide this body, this shame.

Behind him, the two lovers laughed.

Chapter 16

Arvada was mildly surprised to recall just what a desolate place the brig of a fast cruiser was. She hardly ever got down here, in any of her commands. A crew member wasn't doing you much good locked away. There were always extra shifts, always unpleasant jobs looking for repentant hands.

This place looked bleak even for a squared-away fighting ship. Monochromatic. And where the rest of the *Geirovar* smelled almost aggressively clean from the air scrubbers and the maintenance bots, the brig somehow maintained a stale, neglected scent, like a well-used gym. Arvada couldn't see any dust, but could not avoid the impression it was there, probably hosting God knew what microbes.

The room was some twenty meters in diameter, pinched on the back three-quarters by a row of clear plastic-fronted cubicles. They faced a workstation behind which two green-suited members of Security sat on high stools. As Arvada entered they looked so painfully attentive she could tell they were bored out of their minds. That was Security's function. Bored was good. Excited was bad.

The walls were plain blue-gray, unadorned. The prisoner's cell was likewise bare because Arvada had not yet gotten around to offering him any amenities, such as activating the wall screens. Not for two days now, despite Security forwarding a barrage of complaints from their guest. Mostly demanding a computer.

No way in hell was she was going to allow this alien anywhere near a computer. If, as he claimed, the rules of war said otherwise, they could just tack that onto the charge of killing three thousand civilians.

"Wait outside," she told the guards. "Leave visual, kill the audio."

As they exited she went over to the Evolved's cell, in the place of honor right in the center so the guards wouldn't have to strain their necks. Half the cell wall had been grayed over, offering an illusion of privacy. Though the overhead cameras remained on.

The Evolved — Beck — rose from his chair, swiveling aside the screen integral to all the cells. She'd allowed him free run of the *Geirovar's* library of literary and musical works. He could select titles; no other input was operative. Maybe he'd finish reading *Gulliver's Travels*.

He advanced to the other side of the glass. He wore standard naval magenta fatigues. The color suited his tanned skin (natural, or acquired? Why?). The guards had provided him a grooming kit, and he'd made good use of it. His chestnut, earlobe-length hair was swept back from a wide, somewhat aggressive forehead in thick waves. His taut, leathery cheeks were glass-smooth. For some reason Arvada had imagined the Evolved would have discarded facial hair, but the guards informed her otherwise.

His ascetic good looks and close-mouthed, demanding visage would have been perfect for the head of some middling-grade commercial enterprise; a man who substituted drive and avarice for native ability. Only in

Beck's case she imagined innate self-righteousness outweighed any personal greed. Once again Arvada was surprised, and somewhat disappointed, to see how purely *human* he looked. But the Evolveds' emphasis was on the mental, not the physical. It would be unwise to underestimate him.

Thankfully, however, there was no need to strain herself pretending she didn't dislike him personally, and find his whole race loathsome. She'd been warned against such dehumanizing attitudes at the Academy. Being declared a war criminal freed you from a lot of diplomacy.

Viewing the monitors in her cabin, Arvada thought she'd detected signs of an incipient twitchiness. Suppressed, perhaps illusory; when she tried to define it all she really saw was a perhaps exaggerated stillness.

Time to rattle his cage.

So here she was, looking for ways to stick pins into him. Pity Sahan could not be here; he had a near-preternatural ability to infuriate anyone. Her most of all. But she'd definitely picked up a wrinkle or two from the master.

"Hello," she opened.

For a moment he stood opposite her in perfect stillness. Literally perfect. Not a bad trick; Sahan, with his years of standing meditation, could do it, and Arvada sometimes. Not as good as Beck.

"I do not really expect to alter your behavior," he announced, "but in strict accordance with the rules of war as codified by your own Peregrine Alliance, I must formally protest my treatment in the gravest possible terms."

"Gravest possible terms? And what would those be?"

"I believe my meaning is clear."

"I'm just wondering. Inhumane? Unspeakable? Barbaric? Oh no, don't call me *insensitive*. That would be just too crushing."

"Having for the moment secured the upper hand, you mock both legality and common humanity. You make quite the fetish out of being a pirate queen, don't you, *Captain* Sattar." The venom in that "Captain" could have poisoned a whale. "Yet is this truly the wisest course for both yourself and those who — for the moment — place their trust in you? The fortunes of war can be fickle. For instance. Has news that the Citizens' Council declared you a war criminal reached your fleet yet?"

"We're having a party to celebrate. Since surrendering so many of our ships, the Council's opinions are held in roughly the same esteem as Raisa Catalan's. And yours, of course. I'll try to save you a piece of cake. That is, if I can keep those gluttons from the *Anata* from gobbling down everything in sight."

The true answer was no, the fleet hadn't heard. Arvada would either cross or burn that bridge when it materialized before her.

"One thing puzzles me, though," she said. "Why would you believe a war criminal would be influenced by the rules of war? Some convoluted chain of logic I am too un-evolved to understand?"

His perfect stillness showed just the slightest shifting of weight on the soles of his feet. If she hadn't spent so much time training in the martial arts, she would not have picked it up.

"Very well," he said. "Set aside legality. Just how long do you intend to keep me in this demeaning and wholly inhumane condition?"

"Till the war is over, I should think. Or the *Geirovar* is destroyed. Which come to think of it, would be pretty damn dire for you, wouldn't it?"

"What are you trying to say?" Was that just the slightest hint of a snarl roughening his mellifluous baritone?

"If you go down with the ship, with no Master Holobrain to usher you through the Terror Barrier, then you'll be marooned there, won't you? Until the holobrains themselves cease to exist. Or beyond that, even? Like, the life of the universe? Sahan wasn't sure. But he kept having to fight off attacks from the Evolved he killed at Q-89, so he got a pretty good look at just where you're headed if you die. I can see why you want me to restore you to your own people. Which is exactly what handing you over to the Citizens' Council would amount to."

Were his lips starting to work together? Fantastic. She'd have him bouncing off the walls before she was through.

"Only even nestled in the bosom of your own kind," she said, "you can still get killed. As I believe Sahan and I have demonstrated. So you're still facing the Terror Barrier. Unless you have another one tucked away? No, you people have circled the wagons too tight for that. *Or*" — hell and damnation — "is a replacement on its way?"

"You don't actually expect me to answer that, do you?"

"Not at this time, no. Maybe as the days wend by, you'll be more forthcoming. How do you like your new home, by the way? Everything to your satisfaction?"

She wished the cell had iron bars. She was sure his knuckles would be turning white around them.

"This ... is unconscionable."

"Why would you expect a war criminal to have a conscience?"

He took a deep breath, held it a moment, and blew it out in one harsh expulsion.

"I would remind you," he said, "that despite your obviously forced show of bravado, you may one day be judged by my people, apart from your own."

"I doubt it. I'm more of the 'victory or death' type, myself. But even if so, what are they going to do? Condemn me to the Terror Barrier? Oh, but they can't, can they? I don't have a preexisting bundle of memories fermenting or whatever it is they do in the Master Holobrain. You, on the other hand" — ¬¬she faked a shiver — "it's just too terrible to think about. And I don't even like you."

She gave a start as his fist hammered the glass. Despite its strength it quivered, shimmering his image.

"*Are you really so dead to all morality?*"

This was more like it. The cage was getting well and truly rattled.

"Tell me exactly what you need," she said, all business now. "Not who you want me to surrender you to. That's not going to happen."

"That's the only way it *can* happen."

"I'm still listening. For a while."

He pressed his fingertips to the plastic. Scratched down. No sound came through, but so squeezed was his expression that Arvada imagined a squeal anyway.

"I need a holobrain," he told her. Weariness, and just maybe a touch of fear, marred the Superman persona he'd tried to maintain. "Not necessarily so very close. But within the same star system, at least."

"And if you don't have it?"

"If I don't have it ... *you are torturing me!*"

His head drooped; for the first time since they'd met he did not stare her straight in the eye with challenge aforethought.

"Tell me about it."

"Will it make any difference?"

"Depends what's in it for me, doesn't it?"

"You can see I am in pain."

"So am I. Pain happens, in war."

"No pain you can experience can possibly compare to this!"

Rage came abrupt as a blow to the solar plexus. For a moment, she couldn't speak. She saw Sahan clear in her mind. So clear. As if she could touch him. But they would never touch each other again.

It passed. The moment, not the rage.

"I'm just too primitive, huh? The higher emotions beyond me?" Plans formed in the back of her mind. Random noises, flashing lights, sleep deprivation ... like rank, being a war criminal hath its privileges.

"I didn't mean that," he said quickly. Amazingly, he sounded contrite. "Just that my pain is of a different ... composition."

"Enlighten me."

A look of petulance crossed his face as Beck teetered on the brink of another outburst. But after a perilous few seconds, sense prevailed. He gave a sigh, and resigned, began to open up to her.

***

"We are not a people who can well tolerate mental isolation," Beck told Arvada from behind the clear plastic partition of his cell. "We — those of us existing outside the Master Holobrain—"

"The living, you mean?" That was Sahan's idea.

"It is your own intelligence you insult with such petty simplifications."

"I stand corrected."

"We do not share the true Group Mind. Yet we do communicate with what you call the Master Holobrain. Which is a wholly inadequate term for...."

"For God?" she suggested, as he grasped for language suitable to the grandeur of his subject.

"Don't mock something you cannot understand!"

"Do you?"

That fetched him up. "Not in its entirety. Not from outside; no one can. I, as one whose experience of the holobrain is so painfully incomplete, can only try to explain the barest outline to you, whose experience is non-existent."

True enough. But Arvada would bet that Sahan could have taught Beck a thing or two about holobrains that would astonish him.

"As simply as I can express it," he said, "the Master Holobrain is a form of collective consciousness forged from the lives of those who came before, and whose memories were transcribed within. Mainly in real time. Though incorporated into the Group Mind, these individuals retain their own distinct awareness, just as in life."

"How can you know?"

"We know. We do communicate with them. It is true that we cannot participate in the simultaneous communication they enjoy. Human brains did not evolve the complexity necessary to comprehend such a flood of simultaneous impressions.

However, after long practice, we can understand specific directives. As can the subsidiary holobrains."

"So how is that different from a computer?" Arvada asked.

"A computer does not rip your mind apart if you read its machine language." He shot her a look of contempt, quickly wiped from his face. "My apologies, Captain. Your question struck me, likely erroneously, as a deliberate provocation. So I made a facetious reply. Please understand that for us, these matters invoke the same awe and respect as religion among many humans. The basic level of communication I described is merely an exchange of data. It does not begin to convey an accurate impression of our deeper relations with the holobrain."

"My apologies in turn. I meant no disrespect." Not too much, anyway.

"For us," Beck continued, "our union with the Master Holobrain does not involve direct language, nor communication with any of the individual voices that make up the Group Mind. It is ... how to convey this? A sensation. A feeling of inclusion in something so vast as to encompass the universe. Which I know must strike you as fanciful, but that is what we feel. A wholeness. An underlying, all-inclusive truth just beyond reach, yet waiting for us when we join the collective. A sensation too of the collectivity of time. That is, that all events throughout history are but variations on the same moment.

"Please do not ask for a more precise explanation. I cannot furnish one. That being the problem of mystics throughout human history. But this is not mysticism. *This* is real. The array of, of voices, of memories, of experience, all contained in one supreme realization, pulls to every fiber of mind and body.

If we could but assimilate it. Yet even to stand on the edge, staring into the grand mystery we know will be revealed when we join the fellowship of the holobrain, *that*" — he panted for breath, overcome — "is a glory beyond all imagining to those who have not...."

With a start he came back to the distinctly non-transcendent confines of the brig, remembering he was talking to one of those who indeed had not come even close.

For all Beck's absorption in his own vision, his account was hardly so novel to Arvada as he might have imagined. Indeed, it stirred up most vivid images of Sahan and his various invocations of "the pure white light." Mostly Sahan stayed self-conscious and reticent about this mystical side of his being, which brought with it wisps of the Dainichi. Every now and then, though, he would ... tell? confess? to Arvada some of the sensations he'd experienced during meditation or Tai Chi. Moments of ecstatic awareness that formed and burst quick as bubbles.

For Sahan, combat and the quest for transcendence were not separate endeavors. Though his success had been much more apparent in the former.

Sahan, she thought, if I could wish one thing for you, it would be that in your moment of sacrifice, you achieved the vision you pursued all your life.

"But it is my understanding," she told the still awe-struck Beck, "that there now exists no Master Holobrain anywhere within the Peregrine system. Or am I misinformed?"

He hesitated. "You cannot possibly expect me to answer such a question."

She shrugged. "Depends what you want from me. Or more precisely, how badly you want it."

"To inflict pain in order to extract information constitutes torture under any definition."

"At the moment," said Arvada, "I'm just trying to understand the nature of this 'torture' you claim to be suffering at my hands."

"You are indeed a sadist." He closed his eyes, regaining his bearings. "Even without what you call the Master, the subordinate holobrains facilitate communication between us. Of a special sort."

"Like telepathy?"

"It is not telepathy, though to an outside observer it might appear so. We can achieve a certain level of communication through the auxiliary holobrains. Which involves impressions and emotions more than words. The degree of actual communication varies. But just the sense of others close by—"

"Close by in your mind?"

"Yes, though in terms of the actual experience it extends beyond that. Or feels that way. It is profoundly ... comforting."

"And without it?"

"The isolation is equally profound. Eventually more so. In extreme cases, it can disintegrate the personality."

"Drive you mad, you mean."

"Yes," he agreed reluctantly.

"Well, that sounds gloomy, doesn't it?"

"Are you looking forward to it?"

Arvada shrugged. "I can take it or leave it alone."

Though in truth she did not want to see Beck disintegrate before her eyes. Suffering for no reason disturbed her. Inside her there remained something of the little girl appalled to learn the universe was not after all universally benign.

"You could prevent it," he pointed out, "by turning me over to your people aboard the *Kepler*."

Arvada ignored that. "Saying, just for grins, we actually had a holobrain. Right here aboard this ship. Besides being all warm and snuggly for you, how could I keep you from communicating to your friends everything you picked up about the Alliance?"

He gestured at the walls. "Such as the color of the cells, or the nature of the food you serve prisoners?"

"How would I know you could not somehow interface with this vessel's computer systems? The holobrains do that aboard your own ships, to they not? And the habitats they occupy? Why was Sahan able to enter the holobrain aboard the *Eustella* to disable the auto-destruct you and your 'civilized' brethren put in place?"

"I do not know what Sahan Kotori did. That is the truth. It was something of a mystery even to the Master Holobrain. He entered through the Terror Barrier, we know that much. How he got out, I at least have no idea. But he was not sane. He could not have been. I cannot penetrate anywhere near so far into the holobrain. None of my contemporaries can.

"As for affecting your computers, the interface between the holobrains and our Artificial Intelligence has been decades in the development. Your own computer systems can no more react to emanations from the holobrain than you can. Perhaps given a computer I could hack into your systems and extract some fragments of intelligence. To communicate anything so exact to the holobrain is beyond my skill. If I could, only a new Master Holobrain could interpret it."

Arvada relished the desperation in his voice. Desperation was the stepping stone to truth. Suffering *for* a reason she did not mind anywhere near so much.

"So if I carry you around with me and no holobrain is forthcoming, what happens?"

"Eventually, and I regret I cannot give you an exact timeline, I will cease to function. You can maintain me on artificial life support for a time. Again, I cannot be specific. But sooner or later I will die."

"And be caught inside the Terror Barrier."

He controlled himself with a visible stiffening, causing him to sway, just slightly, on his feet.

"Possibly."

"And just where would I get a holobrain? I've had one or two, but one got blown up and the other in a misguided moment I turned over to Naval Command for research. I suppose it's back in your people's hands by now. These things are not so easy to come by. So much as it hurts me to say this, it looks like you're just going to have to tough it out."

"Captain—"

She turned and started for the door. She hadn't learned as much as she might have wished, but the interview had not been entirely without profit. Let's see what he had to say in another few days.

As for the possibility of Beck dying, Arvada had to admit she would not wish eternity in the Terror Barrier on anyone, even an Evolved. But if he was going to get that distraught about it, he shouldn't have blown up his ship.

"Captain Sattar!"

She slowed, hesitated, turned. This had better be good.

"Sahan Kotori," he said, the appeal naked in his sweating face.

Her whole body shimmered in waves of heat.

"Be very, very careful," she warned, "what you say next."

"He is not dead."

A hammer struck her heart. She swallowed, trying to catch her breath. The depth of her reaction was pathetically obvious, but beyond her ability to hide.

"Go on."

"Seconds after his ship tore itself apart, we pulled his body from the solarsphere. His body, I'm afraid that was too badly damaged by heat and radiation to be salvaged. But his brain — part of his brain at least — is being reconstructed."

No. Oh no. No.

Oh Sahan. Oh my poor Sahan. I wished you peace, at least. Yet even now it remains beyond you.

"Reconstructed?"

"I know very little about that. They have sent his brain back to the homeworld. The facilities are better there."

"And will ... he, return?"

"I imagine so. I don't know for sure, but why would they go to the trouble if not to make some use of him? But how or when, I honestly can't tell you. But if he still lives, as I believe, it might be possible to...."

"Yes?" If you're lying I will beat you to death. And if you wind up in the Terror Barrier for all eternity, that will teach you to tell the truth next time.

"That if you get me access to a holobrain, I might be able to learn what's happened to him."

What's happened to him.

Sahan.

Sahan!

Fairy tale. All one horrid fairy tale. Once more she turned, but only halfway. She hung there, unable to make herself leave.

"Captain Sattar! Hear me out, please. I may — and I'm being honest here, Captain, I only say 'may' — be able to make contact with him."

Chapter 17

The milling Grinders had him backed against the wall. They jostled each other as they pressed forward, snarling yet still hesitant, drooling from oversize teeth and bulging jaws. Forty of them, maybe more. Soon they'd sweep over him.

They stood in a military-style dining hall, rows of folding benches with leg flanges bolted to the floor. The bolted-down tables, along with the over-bright lights glinting off gray steel walls, the reek of antibacterials and ozone, and that thick-air atmosphere of inertial dampers, rather like dragging balloons underwater, told him they were aboard a ship.

He kept his back to the wall, swiveling and snarling himself to warn them off. That wouldn't work much longer.

On impulse he looked down to check his body. Human. Of course. Dressed in green fatigues, as were the Grinders facing him.

Why had that been a question?

A Grinder edged in close, blocky teeth bared. Taller and broader than the others. Its skin glinted alternate shades of gold and green under the harsh lights. As the jaws of a human skeleton often seem more prominent than in life from the paucity of flesh and the outsized, hollow sockets above, so the Grinder's prominent mouth and jaws rendered the upper face skeletal. In its large dark eyes, taller than they were broad, the man saw twin reflections of himself.

Then consciousness wavered. A profound sense of displacement swept over him.

Suddenly he understood why the Grinders had such trouble gathering their courage to attack one man.

He was Sahan Kotori.

Of course he was. He knew that; he'd just forgotten somehow. Only now he was looking at Sahan Kotori from the outside, as the Grinders saw him. Superimposed over the image of the man standing with his back to the wall came scenes of battle. A power-suited figure he knew to be himself slashed his way through parties of Grinders in unstoppable flurries.

The images came from the *Enodia*. The massacre in Sector Seal 2-3.

Sahan Kotori alone had fought his way through. Then later invaded the holobrain. The holy of holies.

The Grinders knew all this. Clearly this figure they faced, Sahan Kotori, was more than human. Now he confronted them, and they had no idea of his limitations. The fear of the unknown held them back.

He did not deduce this. He *perceived* it from inside their heads, as he saw the man — himself — defying them.

A new perception crashed into him, along with a new wave of emotion that quivered his legs

ARVADA!

Once more back in his own head, he cringed.

But this time no pain came.

Just a searing wave of hate.

She was responsible for putting him here! She'd set all these Grinders between him and her to block him from his revenge.

Fool! he screamed at her. *Nothing* can keep me from you. Whether dead or alive, for I am Sahan Kotori.

The breath panting from the forbidding mouth of the Grinder less than two meters away smelled of rot and alcohol. Its skin bore a musty scent, not over strong, overlain by the sharp astringency of viscera.

Sahan could all but see straight into the Grinder's head as it eased forward, tempting Sahan to leap at it. Hoping its own reflexes were good enough that it could cover up long enough for its friends to take him from either side.

The Grinder stood directly between Sahan and his revenge.

Watch, Arvada.

His right fist snapped out and back in a vertical punch as he slid his right foot forward. Had the Grinder possessed super-human reflexes, faster than a fifth of a second, say, he might have been able to at least turn his face.

He didn't.

Instead, his head rocked back and his body followed. The two to either side made a vain grab for Sahan as he rushed into the gap, finishing the reeling Grinder with a punch to the throat.

The Grinders behind had been hoping they wouldn't have to exert more effort than squeezing in to stomp on a prone but hopefully still wiggling victim. The falling body knocked them back into each other, raising their hands in a cringing rather than combative posture. In just about exactly a second, give or take a tenth, two of them were dead.

Sahan whirled toward one of those who, failing to grab him the first time, lunged forward for a second try. Sahan deflected his charge to the side and broke his neck as he went by.

There were now four Grinders on the floor, three dead and one balled up and groaning. Sahan stood behind the low barrier formed by the bodies. Hatred burned so hot within him it threatened to raise him from the ground.

ARVADA!

The rest of the Grinders did a surprising thing.

They backed away.

Sahan felt the aggression drain out of them.

Weirdly, it flowed out of him at the same time.

What was going on?

In another surge of displacement, he saw himself once more from the Grinders' perspective.

But ... impossible.

He came back to himself. Looked down to be sure.

Arvada, what trickery is this?

His body was that of a Grinder.

Chapter 18

THEY CAME OUT OF Jump fast and hot, blazing through the white flames of Erigone. Cruiser after cruiser, flanking five heavy ships of the line. Captain Arvada Sattar led the pack in the *Geirovar*.

Three planets out from Erigone the double cylinder *Kepler*, nominal headquarters of the Peregrine Alliance, orbited a mineral-rich but atmosphere-deprived planet. Even on high magnification the habitat showed as no more than a faint red blur of heat amid the star-draped bridge screens. Even more faint came the Collaborationist fleet now claiming sovereignty over the Alliance. Their radio traffic, heat signatures, and exhaust flow showed them patrolling in a loose sphere around the habitat.

They'd be forming up in a hurry.

Coming out of Jump Arvada did not wait for her ships to assemble in battle order. Instead she streaked straight for the enemy, the stream of fast cruisers in her wake.

Such balls-to-the-wall attacks were of course part of her legend. The legend which gave a relatively junior Lieutenant Commander effective leadership of the remnants of the Resistance fleet. The formal authority of Naval Command and the Citizens' Council had been discredited by concessions to the Evolved that ended with the destruction of half the

Alliance navy. In the power vacuum that resulted, no other leader inspired a majority of those left to follow.

Only Arvada Sattar. The woman who struck at the enemy again and again while most of the Resistance fleet twiddled its thumbs. The Captain who took not one but two of the Evolved battleships the rest of the fleet had come to regard as impregnable. Though far from universally beloved, Arvada was the only leader whose record and uncompromising determination could inspire others to believe that the war, which had gone so badly for so long, could still be won.

Yet her leadership was far from assured. She could lose it all right here and now. Jealousy among the senior ranks was still rife. Many older Captains longed for a return to the old order. When years of service meant something. When a ship commander's duty was laid down in Regs, unchallenged by the improvisations of war. When "glory or death" was not the tactic of choice. And most of all when twenty-eight-year-old harpies with a death wish were not the new military ideal.

But the muttering went further than the senior ranks. Because Arvada had been declared a War Criminal by the Alliance's own Citizens' Council.

Her minion Sahan Kotori's destruction of the Master Holobrain housed within the torus *Elipida* had thrown the Evolved into disarray. The breakup of the torus had also cost the lives of three thousand Peregrine civilians.

"Civilians" being the word now debated throughout the Alliance. True, the *Elipida* served as the administrative and logistical hub for the Evolved and Collaborationist fleets. Yet most of those who worked there were not formally classified as military personnel, but civilian contractors. Civilians now drifting in clusters of molecules toward Thais, the system sun.

But just how "civilian" were these dead, whose wartime activities consisted of trying to crush the Resistance? Some saw the question in shades of gray, some in black and white.

And even if one accepted the dead's civilian status, was the strike justified or not? If it turned a losing cause into one with a fighting chance, where did one's loyalties lie? To a code that in practice favored the invaders, or to gaining back the freedom so cherished by the Peregrine Alliance?

It was a question still widely debated. Too widely. In a debate that could yet go against her. So Arvada answered as she always did. Fighting.

With the destruction of the Master Holobrain, she'd declared to the fleet, the Evolved were mortally, even immortally, afraid of death. They might flaunt their heavies, but at the first sign of danger, they would run for their very souls. Not just their lives, as she tried to make clear, but their quite literal eternity. Leaving their Collaborationist allies in the lurch. And these, seeing their champions desert them, would likely fight with less than all-out fervor.

Most did not understand. Many did not agree. Arvada claimed to get most of her information about the Evolved from Sahan Kotori. But how trustworthy was his account, or her interpretation of it? Sahan Kotori had gained the reputation of more warlock than soldier. He was also dead, and few besides Arvada mourned him. *This* was a basis for strategic planning?

But not a single Captain, either of the heavies or the fast cruisers, could come up with another plan that inspired even themselves, let alone anyone else.

Some held out even so. But enough finally agreed to provide her with this attack force streaming all-out at the *Kepler* and the enemy fleet surrounding it.

The Collaborationist fleet and Arvada's were fairly evenly matched. Except for the presence of an Evolved heavy, which would require the joint effort of all five of Arvada's own heavies to engage, with the outcome still far from certain. That left the Collaborationists with three heavies to throw in behind their own fast cruisers, which would battle hers in equal numbers.

The test of her authority was already building. Because as the *Geirovar* sped forward, the fast cruisers chasing after, the Captains of the heavies were demanding to know just what the hell she thought she was doing.

"We're getting complaints from the heavies that they're falling behind," reported Ligea Romero, belted into the slightly lower XO's chair on Arvada's right. "That you're splitting the fleet. *Leya, Argo, Dysis*, they're all requesting that we shed velocity and set up an attack formation."

Arvada still got a quick rush of displacement and heartache seeing someone else in the chair Sahan had so long occupied.

She went ship to ship. Like everyone else throughout the attack force, she was suited up, helmet and all. No telling what their bodies might have to withstand. All around the bridge stations, jetpacs and oxy cylinders stood clamped to chairs, ready for quick deployment. Arvada devoutly hoped they'd stay there.

Experience told her there was a good chance they wouldn't.

"This is Force Command," she transmitted, forming the words in her mind. "All ships, proceed forward at flank speed."

Everson Brooks of the *Argo* protested. "Captain Sattar, at flank speed we'll get strung out. The cruisers are already pulling ahead of us. Do you plan to engage the enemy piecemeal?"

Had he not been her senior in rank, by a goodly margin, he would not dare to question her this way. Over an open channel, no less. And Arvada could have slapped him down appropriately.

Unfortunately, she was a Lieutenant Commander and he the most senior Captain in the fleet. She could not afford to thumb her nose at him. Yet.

"I understand your concern, Captain Brooks. However, I do not expect to fight a set-piece battle. Soon you will see the Evolved heavy try to loop around us on its way to the sun to make a Jump."

She'd explained this in greater detail before. Now he and the other heavy Captains would have to take it or leave it. Hopefully not to the extent of abandoning her and the cruisers.

"The Evolved will take a screening force of enemy cruisers with it," she said, "to prevent our own cruisers closing in and fastening to its hull as it comes out of Jump. As the *Geirovar* and her sister cruisers did in our previous engagement."

That was *me*, people. Remember? I've notched two Evolved line of battle ships on my bowsprit. So get your nose out of Regs and listen to someone who's been and done.

"And I would much prefer," she added, "no more ship-to-ship discussion of our battle plans."

The silence was weighty. She could all but feel Everson Brooks digging his fingernails into his palms in his desire to suggest his own plan of battle. So also, no doubt, were some of the others.

Ligea, no fading flower, looked over to her, clearly thinking Arvada was running a bluff and wondering how it would come out. Arvada could see her concern through her helmet.

Well, the die was cast. One advantage of being regarded as a madwoman, not to mention a war criminal, was that no one believed you'd listen to reason.

"Are we all clear on this?" Arvada asked. "Captain Brooks?"

An agonized hesitation. Agonizing for both of them, actually.

"Understood, Captain Sattar. Maintaining flank speed."

If she was wrong....

She could lose the war this very day.

***

The Collaborationist fleet flew straight at them. Leaving the *Kepler* unguarded, which was a relief. Had they threatened to destroy the habitat Arvada was determined to call their (hopefully) bluff, but she didn't know how many of her Captains would have stood behind her.

The huge plow-nosed Evolved ship, with looming cliffs for sides, led the attack. A screen of cruisers enclosed it. The three enemy heavies, even at full speed falling slowly behind, formed a rearguard whether they wanted to or not. More Collaborationist cruisers bridged the lengthening gap between the two forces.

"Are they going to stand and fight?" asked Ligea Romero at Arvada's side. "Or are they going to try to shoot their way through?"

"Neither," replied Arvada.

Requests for instructions came over her command channel. Those from the heavy Captains reflected more urgency than Arvada found seemly. The channel was scrambled, but did they know for certain Evolved AI couldn't decode it?

The gist was that her ship commanders wanted badly to slow their mad rush forward and assume dispositions that stood some chance of meeting the enemy formation in a toe-to-toe engagement.

Arvada was tempted herself. If she was wrong about the Evolved's intentions, the opposing fleet's concentrated firepower as they blew through her strung-out ships could decimate her force in minutes.

"Commander," said Everson Brooks, obviously speaking for the heavy Captains as a group, "if our two fleets meet like this, we will be destroyed. You told us the Evolved ship would swerve to avoid us. He's shown no signs of it so far. If he keeps coming straight on...."

He let it hang there, demanding an answer. A fully committed answer, because she was fully committing her fleet.

Arvada firmly believed the Evolved wanted to avoid combat. But what if her snake-thin formation tempted it to change its plans?

Sahan, she called. Tell me what to do.

It wasn't battle advice she sought. Such decisions she would make on her own. Rather she sought to render his voice once more firm in her memory. She needed to recall, word for word and most especially the tone in which they were expressed, his tortured accounts of invading the holobrain. Of desperate maneuvers within the Terror Barrier, and fighting off the

Evolved he'd killed, who repeatedly tried to drag Sahan down into the depths of unspeakable fear and isolation with him.

She needed to see again the fear that followed him from the Barrier, slowly disintegrating his mind. She needed to feel again her own heartbreak as she watched him tortured by a form of terror evolution had not equipped humans to withstand.

Could she believe the Evolved in charge of the oncoming warship was brave enough to risk that horror? After all, Beck had not chosen to go down with his ship.

"He won't," she told Brooks. "All ships maintain current speed. And maintain radio discipline, dammit. Quit muttering to each other. If my plans change I'll let you know. Sattar out."

Now to wait. Her least favorite part of combat.

Sahan's memory had given her confidence. But Sahan wasn't here.

He isn't dead.

Beck's words. Most likely a ploy. The Evolved prisoner was desperate for a holobrain to cuddle with. So he'd hit upon her greatest vulnerability. So much for the woman of mystery.

He may think he's in agony now, but if he's lying I swear I'll measure down to the millimeter just how far his vaunted evolution has lifted him above the real thing. War criminal? I'm just getting started.

Damn, it was as if her heart was tied to wild horses! Hoping that Sahan might still be alive, yet dreading what that might mean.

"Captain!" cried Tarika Okada from her console at the front of the curved bridge. "The Evolved ship is changing course."

Arvada checked the screens. "I don't see it."

"You won't for a little while yet. But there's a definite deviation in his exhaust trail."

"Thank you, Tarika."

Arvada hadn't realized just how many muscles she'd been clenching. For several minutes she watched the bridge screens anxiously until the depiction of the Evolved ship, actually a reconstruction from numerous data readings overlain by imaging, swung seven degrees, the minimum angle at which the eye could definitely detect a change of direction.

Jubilation sounded over the command channel as the Evolved kept turning to their left. Congratulations poured in.

"Cut the chatter, people," she snapped. Normally you'd think twice, tape your mouth, and duck your head in a bucket of tar before thus reproving senior officers, but this one she'd earned.

The Evolved ship continued to veer. The rest of the Collaborationist ships trailed as best they could, the three heavies trying to regain lost ground by cutting the corner. Arvada ordered Tarika to plot a course some twenty degrees sunward of the enemy's present heading, and to keep adjusting accordingly.

"Okay, everyone, this is Captain Sattar. You should be receiving new course coordinates. These will be adjusted continuously. The Evolved ship is not our target. We will stay between the Collaborationist heavies and the sun. In so doing we will assume a more convergent course, closing our ranks. I expect the Evolved ship to continue at the maximum speed its screen of cruisers can maintain. Then as we close it will make a last dash for the sun, leaving them behind. And beyond range to support the enemy heavies. At that point you all know what to do."

She expected a barrage of questions but they didn't come. The other Captains now acknowledged this was Arvada Sattar's battle to win or lose.

"In the event some of the Collaborationists surrender, do not stop to transfer prisoners. Order their crews to take to escape pods. If they refuse, splash them. We will come back to collect the ships and the pods when the battle's done. All clear?"

Acknowledgement came through the earpieces.

"And now," she said, "for the inspirational speech. I fully expect to win this one. Good hunting." Damn, if I could hug every single one of you and kiss you full on the lips, I would. Apparently the prospect of killing makes me all touchy-feely. "Sattar out."

Sahan, she thought, this one is for you.

Chapter 19

Sahan found himself standing in a Grinder body.

The Grinders menacing him fell back in surprise. Of the four lying at his feet, the last of the living went still. Everything went still.

He was taller and thicker than the others. His green and golden skin, glistening under the harsh lights of the dining hall, glowed brighter than theirs, and the interplay of colors at each shift of his body shimmered vibrantly. His arms and legs, though still slender by human standards, were composed of bands of muscle like the legs of horses.

With the change of body his perspective also shifted. He saw himself through the perception of the Grinders, not directly as through their eyes but as a shared image floating among them. Regal. Beautiful.

Though he experienced this same sense of awe, the still-human part of him saw the same forbidding jaws, the same prominent teeth, half threatening, half comical, the same oversize eyes standing rather than lying across his face, and the same hairless, rounded cranium, and found them ugly and inimical.

Yet even as he watched he found himself coming to appreciate the perfection expressed within the parameters of this form, as an ancient statue might express an ideal just beyond reach of human reality. The reverence the Grinders displayed toward the figure infiltrated his own consciousness, instilling the desire to live up to the dream even while still regarding it as something outside himself.

But not so very far, and steadily closing the gap.

Easing his transference into this new form and this new role was his physical comfort in the form he'd taken on. He remembered, vaguely, a long succession of dreams in which he struggled to control his own limbs, progressing only slowly from floundering to clumsy. And this after spending so much of his life bringing body and mind, external and internal, into harmony.

Now he felt all that inner grace he'd once prized once more ordering his limbs. Energy, that he had known as *chi*, pulsed within him, bubbling up from feet rooted deep in the ground. His muscles hung relaxed, yet toned to activate the impulse that would harness broad swaths of muscle fibers into a single movement. His mind stood poised, displaced from all personal concerns as it focused on a broad perception of the moment.

This was the culmination of all those endless, frustrating dreams.

The Grinder flesh called to him of a new destiny. To the Grinders, he was a sort of Avatar.

With that doubled perception that brought him into their minds he felt, literally, their confusion and lingering dread give way to awe.

They fully accepted that he was Sahan Kotori, their most feared human enemy. Having established that, most Peregrines would insist that his current appearance as a Grinder must be an illusion, whether mental or physical.

The Grinders, however, had no problem accepting that Sahan Kotori had been reborn as an idealized version of themselves, in order to lead them to victory. The transformation merely recast an already pseudo-mythical human demon into a pseudo-mythical Champion of their own. Where most humans would have fixed on the contradiction, for the Grinders it was the *mystery* that awoke their wonder and their fealty.

Sahan gloried in the role of demi-god conferred upon him.

This was strength!

More importantly, this was revenge.

His new form might be repulsive to human eyes, but Sahan found himself well pleased.

"ARVADA!" he screamed, hate driving the curse like a hurricane from his throat.

All around him the Grinders bellowed and stamped in response, adding their rage to his own.

Chapter 20

"CAPTAIN?" SAID LIGEA ROMERO, over the channel reserved for the XO. "We're getting awfully deep."

"Acknowledged, Number One."

Arvada was surveying the same numbers on the console of her Captain's chair. Radiation was building toward levels where they'd soon all need a good long unpleasant course of treatment. Everyone aboard ship wore power suits, which helped a bit, but that tide was turning.

In the service it was coming to be said that before boarding Arvada Sattar's ship, be sure to make your deposit at the sperm and ovum bank. She and the late unlamented Sahan Kotori had virtually invented the tactic of hovering well beyond all sanctioned depths in the solarsphere of stars to throw off enemy sensors. Though she'd scored several spectacular victories, it was a place where consensus in the Alliance fleet was that her luck had to run out soon.

Now all along the front of the circular bridge the crew sitting at their consoles carried on an intermittent twitching at the *Geirovar's* grim whale-song of moans and staccato clicks as the hull flexed in Erigone's gravity field. As for the engines—

A flashing light on her console indicated Engineering earnestly sought a word. In private. Arvada mentally voiced *Engineering Level One.*

"Yes, Malaika," she said into her helmet. Malaika Rivera had followed her as Chief Engineer from the *Viveca*. Which surprised Arvada until she realized there'd been no other postings available.

"Captain, heat and gravitational pressure are past all experiential data for this class of ship. And far past proscribed levels. This close in, gravitation and heat levels themselves are unstable. A spike could easily kill the engines due to cavitation in the fuel flow. As could simply staying here too long."

"Thank you, Malaika. I have every faith in you." Rivera had always been a bit fussy for Arvada's taste, but if anyone better understood the inner workings of a fast cruiser, their Captains were holding them under armed guard.

"Captain, I must emphasize," Malaika persisted, having failed to convey sufficient urgency, "the longer we stay at this depth, the greater the odds the engines will fail. It's not *if* so much as *when*. And if they do fail, there is no chance at all we will be able to restart them. Not at this depth."

"We won't linger here much longer, Engineering," Arvada promised, fingers crossed. "Thank you for the heads-up. Sattar out." A simple "acknowledged" would have sufficed, but since Arvada's past behavior already had the Chief Engineer's fingernails chewed down to the quick; she figured she owed her politeness, at least.

In her chair next to Arvada, Ligea Romero spoke once more on their private channel. "How long can the *Filia* hide at such a depth? And if she's either gone on down or slipped away, how will we know?"

Meaning: how long do you intend to risk the ship chasing phantoms?

That was the question, wasn't it?

The battle against the Collaborationist fleet had gone surprisingly close to the way Arvada drew it up. The Evolved heavy made a threat charge that Arvada ignored, though her Captains grew nervous. Then when the Alliance ships didn't open the way to the sun, the Evolved swung wide at full throttle in an effort to dodge around them to reach Erigone and Jump trajectory. The ship may have carried no more than one living Evolved. But however many, they did not care to venture their lives at any odds

Neither would Arvada, if something like eternity in the Terror Barrier awaited her.

The flight of the Evolved line of battle ship left the rest of the Collaborationist fleet drawn out and vulnerable at every point. Their three heavies lagged far in the rear, deprived of any cruiser screen to jam enemy sensors. Arvada's five heavies flew straight into them while she and her cruisers engaged their counterparts, who though having a few more ships numerically, were spread all to hell and gone. Some rushed after the Evolved to maintain the screen, or perhaps save their own skins. Others streamed pell-mell back toward their heavies for mutual support, while still another group tried to assemble a coherent formation with which to meet Arvada's attack.

The Evolved must have exercised total command before the battle. When it ran away, it either failed to establish a new central authority, or in its absence, no one cared what it might have to say.

Though Arvada's cruisers were still pursuing several of the enemy, the main battle was now over. Catalan's fleet — pity she wasn't in it, choosing to huddle instead in the shelter of the three Evolved heavies still at Harrar's Reach — lost one heavy destroyed and another captured, in much battered condition. Arvada's heavies were all still flying, though two of them, Everson Brooks' *Argo* and Deshaun Iago's *Parthenia*, barely.

The cruiser battle had turned heavily in Arvada's favor. The *Geirovar* herself exploded the *Helle*, something that brought Arvada considerable pangs because she knew a number of the people aboard, including the Captain, Vasily Cassel, who'd mounted a skilled defense in difficult circumstances. Two other enemy cruiser had been destroyed, and two more battered into submission. What might prove even more significant was that another two of the Collaborationist Captains had surrendered without firing a shot. Clearly morale in Catalan's navy was not all it might be.

Arvada lost only the cruiser *Reka*, which she was trying hard not to think about. Besides the two damaged heavies, two of her cruisers were in sad shape and might or might not be salvageable.

Clearly a victory, though a bloody one. The fact that all the dead on both sides were Peregrines stifled Arvada's exuberance.

That the Evolved ship had escaped unscathed also dimmed the victory. Strategically, however, the fact that it had deserted its so-called allies would do nothing to increase the Collaborationists' loyalty to either the Evolved or Raisa Catalan. Nor would the casualty figures comfort those at Harrar's Reach who'd backed the Evolved because it seemed either the more self-serving or the less bloody alternative. The Evolved might still rule, but more and more through coercion only.

The Resistance was growing in the Reach. Even among those who did not yet dare voice their beliefs.

So, a victory. But not, to Arvada's mind, yet complete.

Because the third Collaborationist heavy, the *Filia*, had plunged deep into Erigone's solarsphere.

The *Geirovar* followed close after as the pursuing Alliance heavies *Dysis* and *Leya* pulled out of their dives. Normally it would be foolhardy for a cruiser to engage a capital ship. But according to the Captains who'd chased her into the sun, the *Filia* had suffered "significant, possibly fatal" damage.

Arvada knew that Captains throughout history tended to err on the side of optimism in these matters.

But now the *Filia* had vanished from the *Geirovar's* sensors.

Had she pulled out of her dive in time? Established a tangential course, maybe, and made her Jump?

Arvada didn't think so. Not at this depth. To try to break through the gravity at this level would require a commander even crazier than Arvada. And she was morally certain the Collaborationists harbored none such.

Could the *Filia*, already crippled according to some accounts, have failed to pull out from her dive in time? Did the majestic line of battle ship now exist as no more than a crumpled armful of metal and flesh sinking toward where even this would be pulled apart into its component atoms?

That's what Ligea Romero thought. That's what Solange O'Grady and Ayama Cleave, who'd judged her plunge too severe for their own ships to follow, thought.

It was pretty much what Arvada thought herself.

But what if the ship had pulled out in time? She'd been levelling out when the *Geirovar's* sensor readings blurred from hazy to a matter of opinion.

Arvada swallowed a snarl, thinking she should have followed deeper after her prey. But the *Filia's* crush depth exceeded that of the *Geirovar*. And though the cruiser was faster, the heavy possessed more raw power, what the engineers called "torque" though it had nothing whatsoever to do with tangential forces, with which to claw out of Erigone's gravity well.

What kept Arvada here endangering ship and crew was the thought, less a calculation than an itching unease, that the *Filia* might still be lurking below. Waiting for a chance to surface to a reasonable height, and before the Alliance fleet could pounce, accelerate into Jump.

That would furnish Raisa Catalan and the Collaborationists, along with their Evolved masters, a victory narrative of their own. A morale boost to offset the losses they'd suffered. And maybe even deflect attention from the way the Evolved ran out on their so-called allies.

The pedestal was all prepared.

Arvada meant to crumple the statue they'd set upon it.

***

He awoke in strange quarters, after an obscure but troubling series of dreams.

Dreams that though now only fragmentary and disconnected, possessed the nagging weight of memories.

He lay on his side, perfectly still, eyes closed, as always when waking. Listening for the sound of intruders, silently establishing contact with his limbs to be ready for sudden, all-out action. While no such attack had ever happened, not at least in his present memory, a history of troubled dreams had long made him alert.

He first knew the room was new to him because the bed was different. Harsh, yielding stubbornly directly beneath the point of pressure, forcing the rest of the body and limbs to bend to fit. The pillow was no better. He'd placed his head near the edge to avoid scrunching his mouth, nose, and neck.

None of this bothered him. His body, which also felt strangely new to him in many ways, possessed the same firm pliability it always had.

Sahan Kotori, he said to himself.

It felt right, and yet....

He had the same trouble fitting his memories to the name as his body to the mattress. They, or his dreams — or hallucinations? — covered too large a span to coordinate themselves within a single narrative.

The room was larger than most quarters he'd known. He could feel this even through closed eyes. Faint sensations like a disturbed breeze bounced back from the walls to caress his face. As he tried to trace them, the dimensions of the room itself began to shape themselves in faint shades of blue-gray. The images did not appear on the backs of his eyelids, but toward the center of his head.

Echo-location? But he wasn't wearing a suit.

Reflexively he swallowed to relieve the dry mouth of mornings.

Only there was no dryness. No sour taste. Just a strangely abstract mechanical reflex.

Nor did he feel any pressure from his bladder.

His eyes snapped open as unease began to build.

The room was dark. His eyes saw nothing.

Except the blue shades deep inside his head, outlining walls, chairs, a desk or dining table ... and a console faintly outlined in red from the electrical activity inside.

Infra-red.

He wiped a hand across his eyes to be sure he wore no visor or goggles. Nothing. He was a Grinder. He'd been a Grinder ... yesterday? — when the others all hailed him. A Grinder, bigger, stronger, quicker, and of stronger will than they themselves.

Yet that was the thing.

This wasn't a body after all.

He felt touch, sensation, movement, pain. He *felt* possessed of a genuine body.

So long as he did not look beyond the emotions that usually preoccupied him.

But quiet the mind, reach out a little further, and the body vanished.

It was a purely mental construct. Or rather, it was a mechanical sheath of incredible verisimilitude. If not smoke and mirrors, alloys and electronics brought to what must be the brink of vitality. Why, just thinking of movement, if no more than lifting a hand, he marveled at how instinctive the action felt.

Of course nerves, including brain cells, had long been used to control muscles through artificial electric stimulation. But precise, wholly natural perceptions of pain, proprioception, a direct internal sense of balance, not to mention such instinctive control over your body as to perform Tai Chi (though he seemed to recall it had taken him a frustratingly long time to learn) these were still far beyond the reach of Peregrine technology.

A marvel indeed.

But still artificial. Everything was artificial but his brain.

You'd think that when he so triumphantly asserted himself before the Grinders, he might have noticed a little detail like that. Odd thing to slip your mind. Yet he'd watched the Grinders, performing their parts in this miracle play the Evolved staged for them, proclaim him their leader, their demi-god, and take his vengeance for their own. While all the time he believed himself one of them, if only by adoption.

He had not questioned his transformation from the human Sahan Kotori to an idealized Grinder. Neither had they. The Evolved possessed too much control over all their minds.

So what about his brain? His thoughts? His memories? Just how much control did he exercise over his own—

PAIN.

He crumpled to the floor as acid burned its way through every nerve fiber, or whatever passed for them, in brain and body.

Whatever you're thinking, he begged his mind, *stop!*

The pain ceased, leaving behind no ache, though he could swear he detected a faint smell of burning. Just a reminder, most likely.

He rolled up into a cross-legged position, amused, in the same fuck-me sort of way he found existing in a mechanical body amusing, to realize he shared his mind with others. The Evolved had affixed positive or negative feedbacks to steer his mind where they wanted.

Just how extensive was that minefield? And what lay beyond?

PAIN.

How the fuck did they find every single neuron in his body, imagined or real, to burn with a cutting torch?

The pain ceased. Just a little reminder to help him establish the boundaries.

Best just settle in for now. His pride might suffer a few bruises knowing free will was something for other people, but hell, by now he ought to be used to it. Had he ever served as a model of independence those years he let Arvada play him up, down, and sideways, laughing at him all the while?

Had he ever once thought he might have a life outside her? Not hardly. Once he realized Arvada would never, ever love him, all that changed was his horizons shrank down to one. To die in her service. Hopefully earning at least a little gratitude at last. Maybe. As time went on the gratitude became less important than the dying. Just to get some rest.

Pathetic.

Whatever else they might have done, the Evolved had at last freed him from her.

So okay. He'd died, in his way. And been reborn. Partly in his way, partly in the Evolved's. Beggars can't be choosers.

Probably better this way, really. The human Sahan Kotori had demonstrated less spine than a nematode in resisting Arvada. Over the years she'd diminished him more and more and more.

So in a way, this was her final victory. Because she couldn't have robbed him of much more.

It would also prove her doom.

Chapter 21

It all depended on whether what Tarika Okada thought she saw on the screens was the *Filia*, a random solar phenomenon, or just wishful thinking.

Arvada gave up trying to interpret her own console as the fuzzy gray blobs transferred from the screen to her eyes. Unbelting herself from the Captain's chair she started toward the curving platform where Tarika, belted in before a massive array of screens, graphs, and dials, supervised the other Signals officers.

Ligea Romero started to unbuckle to follow her but Arvada waved her back into her chair.

"In case we have to do something very fast," she explained.

Like dodge a missile rising up from the impenetrable (to their sensors, anyway) depths of the sun. The inertial dampers would hopefully keep everything more or less in place in the event of evasive action. Hopefully. She'd seen it fail. If the *Geirovar* began to buck without enough warning for Arvada to get back to her chair, she might end up bouncing all over the bridge.

The sun's gravitational field, itself shifting with Erigone's rotation and sudden collapses deep within the core, imposed additional strain on the dampers. Gentle currents nudged Arvada this way and that as she crossed the floor. The handbook said such perceptible gravitational waves signified you should have been climbing out ten minutes ago.

She fitted herself in between Tarika and an extremely tight-lipped junior lieutenant Vromme. Lifting off her helmet to get a more direct view, she indicated for Tarika to do the same, with the benefit that they could talk without being overheard or going to the trouble of keying to the same channel.

Lieutenant Vromme followed automatically, revealing his strained breathing and a thin sheen of sweat. Temperatures inside the hull were indeed rising to uncomfortable levels, but not beyond the suits' ability to compensate. Rising up from the open ring around his neck Arvada caught the scent of sweat coppery with fear. Hearing the moans from the straining hull, she imagined them as Vromme's own.

"Show me," she told Tarika. And leaning over Vromme with a hand on his shoulder she whispered: "Exciting, isn't it?"

What was she supposed to say? Don't worry? If that worked she'd be telling it to herself.

Calling up a red flasher on the wide screen before her, Tarika circled an area near the center of the yellow field that to Arvada's eyes didn't look different from any of the rest of the screen. Erupting streams of heat depicted in hard white and magnesium yellow huffed and puffed, elbowing each other aside before ebbing back or, detaching from their stalks, bubbling up to jostle the *Geirovar* and induce a sinister hissing in the engines' hum, along with heart-jarring knocking in the pods from disruptions in the fuel flow.

That was heat.

In a 3-D field underlying the glowing clouds, curtains of mostly dull red, intensifying here and there to carmine, waved in delayed rhythm to the shifting billows of heat.

That was radiation, and the Medical Officer's button was a constant flashing red Arvada had no intention of responding to because she had no answer beyond this is war, dammit.

Green for gravity had been switched off to avoid interfering with Tarika's possible sighting of the enemy heavy. Arvada didn't want to see it anyway. She could hear it as the ship groaned like a ghost with the flexing of the hull.

"I don't see a line of battle ship," she said, after peering so close her nose practically left its print on the screen.

"Nor did I, at first," responded Tarika. "But the AI did. There is a slight, a miniscule, even I suppose an arguable, increase of radiation emanating from that point there." She wiggled the red flasher.

"At what distance?"

"Impossible to tell precisely, Captain. There's just too much background radiation. Saying it does come from a ship's engines, though, it couldn't be that far. Else we wouldn't see even this. Say one hundred kilometers, maybe one fifty at the outside."

Arvada bet there was some sweating going on down there, along with an entire metallic opera from the hull.

"Can they see us better than we can see them?" The answer should be yes, but not by much. Always better to check, though.

"Some, probably," Tarika answered. "We do have a smaller footprint. But if they launch missiles amid such radiation their targeting systems are almost certain to be scrambled long before they draw near."

"Have you shown this to Engineering?"

"Just after telling you."

Arvada clapped her helmet back on and called Malaika. "Do you see what Tarika's pointing at?"

"I'm *kind* of seeing it, Captain."

"Could it be a ship using high thrust to keep from sinking deeper in the solarsphere?"

"Possibly. I'd want to monitor that location for at least another ten minutes or so before committing myself."

Lucky I'm Captain, then.

Or was it? She took a quick scan of the bridge, at the backs of all these suited figures. Was she risking her ship and its people just to notch one more victory in the legend of Arvada Sattar?

She did have that tendency. Sahan had frequently pointed it out to her. But put his life on the line time and again to make it come true. His life, and his mind.

Sahan....

Isn't here. You're on your own.

We can't defeat the Evolved heavies. Especially not without Sahan to work his wizardry in the holobrains. Therefore we must destroy the faith of those Collaborationists still staking their future on them. There was an Evolved heavy here. See what good it did you. Witness its loyalty to its so-called allies.

I will not permit this ship hiding below us, if such it is, to escape and counter that narrative with one of heroic endurance and escape. I will crush them, and I will crush the spirit of those clinging to the hope that the Evolved and Raisa Catalan are their future.

"I know they've got a greater crush depth than we do," Arvada told the Chief Engineer. "But do their engines share a proportional resistance?"

"In truth, Captain," Malaika replied, "no one knows. No Alliance ships have ever operated at these depths before, even in exercises. The critical factor is that their fuel pressure is so much greater than ours at max thrust. They are not immune to cavitations from heat flux, or even gravitational shifts. And I wouldn't think that at this depth their engines could resist cavitations any better than ours. But in theory — and I emphasize that 'theory' — their fuel flow should give them higher survivability at these depths than us."

Arvada did not miss the slight emphasis on 'survivability.'

"However," Malaika continued, "in practice it is my opinion, founded on nothing in particular, that time, that is exposure, will prove the decisive factor. Because the longer either of us lingers here, the greater the chance to encounter a fluctuation that will overwhelm us. Either of us."

What the Engineer was saying was, we could all be doomed at any moment. What Arvada heard was, between them and us, it was a flip of the coin.

In other words, a game of bluff. Or nerve.

"Thank you, Malaika. Keep an eye on things." She switched off the channel but kept her helmet on, signaling Tarika to do the same. Vromme, by now breathing through his mouth, followed suit. Arvada patched in Tarika and Ligea, and put them on a private channel.

"Tarika, I want you to plot a parabolic course. We will dive down on the *Filia* at an angle of forty-five degrees. We will assume she lies one hundred kilometers below. We'll go in at maximum thrust, then begin pulling out where our course will bottom us out fifteen kilometers above the enemy vessel. Which should be more visible to our targeting as we draw closer. If you see her at no more than one-twenty-five klicks adjust your dive accordingly, only bring us out twenty klicks above. If she's deeper, you will still pull out at that same point. We will use the speed generated by our dive to dig out at the optimal angle we can maintain."

"Aye, Captain. Parabolic course, forty-five degrees, bottom out above the enemy." Tarika didn't usually repeat orders just to make sure she had them right. She was giving Arvada a chance to change her mind. And no doubt hoping she would. Arvada herself felt sick with worry, but committed.

"Inform me when all is ready."

Switching back to the channel with herself and the First Officer only, Arvada walked back toward her chair, again swaying slightly in the gravitational currents.

Was she really going to go through with this?

"Are you really going to do what I think you're going to do?" asked Ligea, when Arvada was once more belted in, adding "Captain" somewhat belatedly.

"We can't stay here," Arvada replied.

"Neither can they. Not indefinitely."

"I'm listening, Number One."

"Say we climb a couple of thousand kilometers or so to a safe level. They have to come up some time. Then we can be standing by with the *Argo* and *Dysis* in support."

Arvada had been pondering the same thing.

"It's an attractive idea," she acknowledged. "The problem is that if the *Filia* doesn't come all the way up into confirmable sensor range, but instead breaks off into a tangential course before we pick her up, we'll lose her."

"What I don't understand," said Ligea, "is why she hasn't tried to slip away already. Presuming that is her, of course."

"Because we were too close behind her. Had they attempted to veer away from straight down, we would have traced the disturbance and alerted the whole fleet to her course. Now she's lying-to as deep as she dares go. Deep enough to give the builders fits if they knew. Their Captain has no way of knowing just where we are, or what we're seeing against the background radiation, or if we're definitely here at all. He's hoping we're looking at ghosts. And he may be right. He also knows it was a cruiser last in pursuit, and he'll be thinking we can't lurk here forever."

"So he's trying to wait us out."

"That's his hope. He knows we'll have to rise to a safer level soon. Basically we're both holding our breath. Who will give up first? Our intel says it's Nissim Shakir commanding the *Filia*. He's a serious man, and he knows his ship. His Chief Engineer is probably under sedation. When his instincts tell him he's run out of time, he'll bring her up slowly. If he gets a sensor lock on us he'll shoot off as sharp and fast as he can and hope for the best. But what he wants, short of no one being there, is to climb to a level where gravity will allow him to slide into a rising tangent *before* he comes into range of our own sensors."

Ligea stared at her curiously. "You really can read his mind, can't you?"

"There's only so many things you can do with a ship. And only so many types of commanders. This is a good one."

"I wish to hell he'd just surrender," Ligea said wearily. "I'm sick of killing other Peregrines. I've known too damn many of them. But I don't suppose surrender is in his nature. Any more than it's in yours."

"Then we're locked on course. Tarika?"

"Almost there, Captain."

Among the several lights flashing on her console was Engineering. Leaving Ligea and Tarika Okada both patched in, Arvada responded.

"Yes, Malaika?"

"Respectfully, Captain, I cannot guarantee the functioning of either the engines or the hull itself under the course I've just seen. In fact, I feel compelled to protest."

"Formally?"

Hesitation. "No. But please listen to me, Captain. Picking up this much velocity on our downward dive imposes a definite danger that we will not be able to pull out at the end of it. And the strain on the engines ... we are way far in unknown territory here. Or rather, the only knowns are that on occasion engines definitely *have* failed even under far less strains than these."

"But not all of them, not all the time. Look at it this way, Malaika. One swift dive. We're just dipping our toe."

"If I may be permitted, Captain, we're hanging by our toenails. Head down over a pit of molten lava. Literally."

Arvada had not known the Chief Engineer had such flights of imagery in her. Well, they did say that war sometimes brought out the best in people. She tried to laugh, but found her throat too dry and her chest too tight.

"But you are not registering a formal protest?" What did it matter? If Malaika proved right, they'd all be dead. If Arvada pulled this off, no one would care. Except that she would need a new Chief Engineer.

"It's your ship, Captain Sattar. You've surprised me before. So I would not wish any comments I have made to be taken as more than a caution as to some possible, ah, vulnerabilities."

"Thank you, Malaika. Your advice, as always, is appreciated. Sattar out."

With a long-suffering expression Ligea Romero shook her head. "Do *you* believe your own legend? Or is it just the rest of us?"

Ligea often pushed the edge of ... call it familiarity, though insubordination would not be so very far off, more than Arvada would normally tolerate. But Sahan had championed her, and Ligea was indeed competent, level-headed, and — rather like Sahan — wholly loyal by nature, to those few who could win her respect. Besides, after fucking her last XO, Arvada was in no position to complain of informality.

"I *have* to believe," she replied. Meaning, I sure don't have the nerve to try all these desperate ventures on my own.

Sahan had made it so much easier to believe in herself. Even as he needled her. In fact he'd often infuriated her into upholding her legend, even when her own belief was shaky.

"It's quite a risk to take," said Ligea, "if the *Filia* turns out not to be there at all."

"She'll be there."

Probably.

What if she wasn't? What if Arvada killed the *Geirovar* and everyone aboard chasing shadows on a sensor screen?

Damn her muscles were tight! The tension exhausted her.

"Listen," she told Ligea. "Even if we get within ten or twenty kilometers, with that radiation I don't expect our missiles will score a direct hit any more than theirs. We are going to fire *above* her. Close above as we can."

"That should blind any return fire," Ligea observed.

"It will do more than that. In this atmosphere, the explosions will knock her about. Maybe even force her further down. But in any case, jostle her engines. Even if we don't knock them out, there's a good chance we can start them gurgling. Any turbulence at all, it will sound like a torus quake in there. You can bet Captain Shakir will head straight up fast as he can. Like I would."

"Or straight down."

Arvada hadn't thought her stomach could knot up any tighter. "Or that too."

Ligea gave a slight shiver, barely perceptible in her suit. "I used to think I might make a pretty fair fast cruiser Captain. I've changed my mind, knowing you."

"To hell with that. You'd be damn good. Better than most."

Tarika buzzed and Arvada patched her in.

"Final coordinates plotted, Captain."

"Relay it to Engineering. Keep them updated as best you can. But your priority will be Weapons."

"Understood."

She gave the mental command to put her in touch with Weapons. "We are about to make a dive. Quite a steep one. As we pull out I want every piece of ordinance this ship can launch directed at the coordinates you will receive as soon as we get a better fix. Keep firing until told to cease."

"Acknowledged, Captain."

She went ship-wide.

"This is Captain Sattar. Snuggle in, people. Make sure you're suited up, helmet and all. Say something nice to your eyeballs. Let them know you still love them in case they want to go walk-about. We are about to engage and destroy the Collaborationist line of battle ship *Filia*."

She went back to the channel restricted to Tarika Okada and Ligea Romero.

"Dive! Dive! Dive!"

Despite the inertial dampers she was pushed back until the seat firmed up behind her as the *Geirovar's* engines rose to a roar and and the cruiser pointed her nose toward the sun.

God, she was scared.

And yet ... she lived for this.

Chapter 22

The *Geirovar* swept down through the solarsphere. Arvada stared hard at the seething yellow field on the console before her. A host of highly relevant data was marching across the surrounding screens, and the way the Engineering button flashed red non-stop, a no doubt colorful interpretation awaited her if she would only acknowledge.

She didn't.

The decision had been made. All that remained was the adrenalin rush of one of those last-microsecond banks she was prone to while racing jet sleds: you pulled back on the stick with all your strength even though it was electronically controlled, watched doom slide across the cockpit ever so slowly, and *hoped* you'd make it, since there was bugger-all else you could do now.

Napoleon once said he chose his generals for luck. A lot of people thought that merely a quaint aphorism. Arvada knew better. Whether she would now prove a battlefield genius or a reckless fool depended on 1) whether the line of battle ship *Filia* actually lay concealed somewhere within that boiling incandescent mass below; 2) the *Geirovar* wouldn't scramble her engines pulling out of the dive or fail to pull out altogether; and 3) enemy fire would not rip her guts out as she did.

She squeezed the arms of her chair hard to keep her helmeted face close over the screen even as acceleration shoved her back. Nothing like a slide down a gravity well to build velocity quick.

She still could make out nothing on the screen that looked like it might be a ship.

It *had* to be there.

Then: "We have a read, Captain." Tarika Okada, in charge of the sensors. "It has to be her. Nothing else that big could withstand the pressure down here."

At Arvada's side Ligea Romero pounded her fist on the arm of her chair. "Yes-s-s-s," she hissed.

At once Arvada switched the view on her primary screen to show their course. Against a dark-blue background a yellow line dove like a hawk toward a rather amorphous but definitely palpable deep purple blob. Streams of data, most in high-priority red and flashing frantically, clustered about both ships.

She tasted blood, scented it in her nostrils. Then noticed pain in her lip. She opened her mouth, sticky with dryness, to release it.

She was sweating. During the dive the heat had built to levels that challenged the suits. Arvada hadn't noticed that either.

"Helm on autopilot, backup engaged," Tarika announced as the ship neared her pull-out point.

"Incoming!" shouted Lieutenant Vromme.

Arvada refrained from calling for Evasive Action. At this depth any new gyrations imposed on either the engines or the hull might tear the ship apart.

The *Geirovar* shuddered. For half a second Arvada hoped the worst was past. Then the ship jerked. Hard. She grunted as her waist smashed against the seatbelt before the inertial dampers could dull the shock. Her head did a quarter-turn, settled.

Mostly. The hull teetered on the edge of a see-saw. A tumble here would disintegrate ship and crew. Myriad tight, involuntary moans filled the speakers while everyone waited to learn their fate. The wavering motion pushed past the inertial dampers to inflict varying degrees of nausea on everyone aboard.

Arvada's surroundings had a floating quality to them. Mostly she was aware of a lot of noise. As always when these things— (a peal of metal. Another jerk. Arvada froze, feeling she was about to be dumped from a cart down the side of a very tall building. The ship stabilized. She sucked in a strangled breath.) — happened. Noise, always noise. Arvada divided the noise into two categories. The first and most pressing was the rapidly pulsing *chock-chock-chock*, in rhythm with small but persistent shudders throughout the bridge.

That came from one of the engines.

Settle, settle, settle, she ordered it, though gently, as you might address a snarling dog.

The second category of noise were the demands of the crew over ship-wide channels from bow to stern, demanding orders like any orders she could give at this point would make any difference.

Prioritize.

She didn't need Engineering. They'd only tell her the *Geirovar* was on the edge of destruction and demand she shed velocity to give them a chance to stabilize the fuel flow before cavitations blew the whole housing apart, along with a chunk of the hull.

She didn't need Damage Control. The *Geirovar* would hold together or it wouldn't.

Medical was trying to barge through on the priority channel. Why did they always think their work so damn important they had to *shout* all the time?

The ship was still close to the planned trajectory. Whether or not it was coming apart about their ears they'd know soon.

"Tarika. Do we still have a fix on the *Filia*?"

"Affirmative, Captain." Her voice had turned little-girlish.

"Weapons. We'll be coming out of our dive in seconds. You have the coordinates?"

"Affirmative, Captain," Lieutenant Wainwright replied.

"Remember. When you get the 'Fire' signal it means fire *everything*. And keep firing till we're out of range. Well out of range. We don't get a refund on what we bring back."

"Got it, Captain."

"Good man."

There. Such a simple job, really. Considering all the lives at stake, so terribly simple. Just set your priorities and it all falls in line.

"Pulling out!" shouted Tarika.

Arvada's eyeballs tried to go walk-about.

She was in a cave, serenaded by a giant playing an accordion made of steel plates. And kicking the walls for a drum.

She was being dragged to death over very bumpy ground.

She knew something very important was going on outside but her mind said she was taking things too seriously.

Hostile jaws bit down on her legs — her suit, trying to force blood to her brain.

She forced her eyes open through the bulging pain but still saw the same yellow and red splotches floating across a purple background.

Everything *hurt!*

A new, less jarring but quicker shuddering came over the ship.

Missiles. Outgoing fire.

Arvada snapped to alertness.

On her screen the purple blob representing the *Filia* grew even more amorphous as explosions on or above her sent blast waves of super-heated particles down, shocking her already strained hull and shoving it even deeper into the inferno.

"Incom—!"

Kicking her tail down, the *Geirovar* roared up and away from the killing zone.

Or roared, anyway. Even with the engines giving all they had, and with all the accumulated inertia of the gravity-assisted dive behind it, the *Geirovar* slowed noticeably on her upward trajectory.

Arvada's speakers went into sound-deadening mode as the cruiser kicked sideways so sharply she and everyone else experienced a moment of whiplash-induced shock despite both the dampers' and their suits' efforts to muffle it. The hull wriggled like a fish. Such wobbles! If the ship didn't pitchpole she'd shake herself to pieces.

If only everything would just stop *spinning!*

Chock-chock-chock-chock.

The engines trying to grab a breath like the victim of a heart attack.

"Engineering!" she called, slapping down on the button. Bile streamed scalding up into her throat. She swallowed it. The ship was still fishtailing dangerously. Noise, noise everywhere. A hundred voices all demanding answers, right now. From her.

"Captain!"

Force yourself to sound calm. But God, it was hot! It must be the heat still forcing all these purple and yellow balls across her vision.

"Report, Malaika."

"Captain, we have severe cavitation in Engine Number Two." Malaika paused to gasp in a breath. "We need to shut it down immediately before it blows."

"Can we keep climbing on one engine? We should still have some momentum behind us from the dive."

Pause. "I don't know. I...."

"Understood. Keep Number Two online."

"Captain, if Number Two goes the back-pressure induced by cavitation may tear apart the engine housing. And send us into God knows what gyrations."

"If you shut it down, is there any chance you can bring it back on line again?"

Another, longer, pause. Come on, Malaika, it's not like you birthed it yourself. "At this depth, I don't know that we can."

"Very well. Do nothing except on my command."

Arvada found it hard to devote all her concentration to the engines while *Geirovar* still shimmied so violently she half-expected to see stars overhead as the roof of the bridge tore off.

Noise, so much noise! But she couldn't quiet either the crew or the ship, which was retching violently.

Okay. Okay. Arvada added one more "okay" while breathing into her abdomen. If we *don't* take Number Two offline, it may blow apart. In which case we die.

If we *do* shut down Number Two and the ship starts sinking, we'll never get it started again. If we try to climb out on one engine, at best it will be slow. And since we'll have to push it at red-line-plus, chances are good we'll knock that one out too.

"Malaika, listen. You will leave Number Two online until otherwise ordered.'"

"Ah, Captain? I appreciate it's a delicate decision, but—"

"Sattar out."

Gradually the *Geirovar* steadied out and followed her nose. The violence of the repeated impacts had caused numerous injuries. Medical thought that a big deal. Well, if the ship couldn't climb out it would save them a lot of effort.

Damage Control also seemed to be taking itself very seriously. Why weren't there more *optimists* on this ship?

Arvada fixed her gaze on the schematic showing the ship's agonizing progress up from the depths. Her climb was at both a slower velocity and a more shallow angle than Arvada had hoped.

Some of the crew, with no other immediate responsibilities, would be checking the clocks regularly, telling themselves the cruiser was only some imagined number — five minutes, ten minutes, she doubted many had the fortitude to go all the way to fifteen — from safety. They would force themselves not to look at the clock until they *knew* five minutes had passed. Then give an inward whine of despair and tell themselves the timekeeping machinery must have gone dingo under the strain, to report one minute and seventeen seconds when they knew damn well more time had passed than that.

Yet they were still climbing. Slowly.

So absorbed was Arvada in watching the schematic that several minutes passed before she thought to wonder about the *Filia*. Switching views, she stared intently at the screen, searching for the purple blob that had marked the approximate position of their enemy.

She saw nothing. She thought of calling Tarika for confirmation, but couldn't bring herself to do it.

Filia was dead. Hopefully it was all over; Arvada hated to think of the crew still slowly sinking, desperately trying measures they already knew to be futile while wondering which would kill them first; heat, radiation, or the collapse of the hull.

The same doom that might yet overtake her own crew.

Climb, damn you, climb! Just bring us a little further from the star's core and maybe then we'll be able to shut down Number Two engine before it kills us all.

Though she was Captain and responsible to her own ship's people, and them alone, she was heartsick over the crew of the *Filia*, and the horrible death she'd brought them to.

Chapter 23

Arvada dreaded the meeting. But right now neither she nor anyone else could state with any certainty the command structure of the Alliance fleet. So a meeting must be called.

Once announced, discord arose over the choice of location. Arvada proposed all commanders report onscreen. She hoped to avoid arguments about whose ship should play host, with the heavy Captains insisting that since they had accommodations designed for diplomatic meetings, it must be one of them. Which would create discord right from the start.

She also wanted to avoid the possibility of getting arrested aboard someone else's ship.

Unlikely, but hardly impossible. She was, after all, a war criminal. Declared so by both the Citizens' Council and Naval Command. If any of the heavy Captains who'd followed her at the battle off Erigone now wanted to assert legitimacy within the Alliance — a now dubious legitimacy in the eyes of many but in purely legal terms the only one going — they could start by doing just that.

Most of the heavy Captains she trusted. In fact she was distressed to realize she mistrusted any at all. Everson Brooks, for instance, had fought his ship hard at the battle of Erigone. But he was also the senior Admiral in the current fleet, even if Arvada was its center of gravity. He had long proved touchy about taking orders from a twenty-eight-year-old (no, twenty-nine, remember? You had a birthday somewhere back there) Lieutenant Commander. Solange O'Grady, though a fiery redhead whose stomach for bending tin could not be questioned, had also made a point that Arvada's authority in the recent battle was also most definitely a one-off.

Therefore Arvada absolutely refused to hold the meeting aboard any of the heavies, in effect daring any of the Captains to issue a direct command and see what happened.

None did.

The whole question, though, was ticklish. The cruiser Captains had accepted her leadership long ago. Whatever their personal ambitions, none had the reputation to remotely challenge her. The heavy Captains, on the other hand, had hemmed and hawed their way into accepting her as battle commander on several occasions. Some with better grace than others. But none went so far as to acknowledge Arvada's authority outside the actual engagement.

The whole question hung fire. If battle was forced upon them in their current state, would the heavy Captains follow her at once, without argument? Or would they follow Everson Brooks? Or would the whole Alliance fleet break apart into bickering factions, all doomed?

In the end no formal meeting was ever declared. Instead all the ships that had taken part in the battle off Erigone, and others that wandered in from patrolling the outlying colonies, found themselves voicing opinions, separating into separate cliques with those of like mind, and seeking to convince the others. Until more or less by happenstance everyone wound up on a screen in everyone else's wardroom.

Which of course started out as one big acrimonious Babel, with the heavy Captains trying to throw their weight around and the fast cruiser Captains pretending like they didn't hear.

Eventually everyone recognized that in the end the whole discussion came down to two voices: Arvada's, and Everson Brooks'.

Seizing the initiative while Arvada was still trying to weigh her support, Brooks stated his case calmly but forcefully, as befitted an Admiral who'd fought enough to be respected for more than the insignia on his uniform. He certainly looked the part; square-jawed, silver-haired, with bright blue eyes set off by a traditionally salty weather-beaten face, gained through tanning creams and wrinkles as carefully selected and trimmed as prized flowers.

"Let us first of all acknowledge," he began, "the victories won by Captain Sattar. She has proved herself an innovative and most daring battle leader. One whose voice should receive careful consideration in any Council of War."

Careful consideration, Arvada noted, being a long way from acceptance. Nor had Brooks mentioned Sahan's contribution, which included taking an Evolved heavy and saving the *Eustella* colony.

On the other hand, perhaps the less said about Sahan the better. Because he was the one who had actually blown up the *Elipida*, causing so many civilian deaths. Destroying the Master Holobrain in the process didn't weigh so heavily with most of them because they still didn't understand what it was.

Nor could you mention Sahan's name without dredging up Arvada's own responsibility for that incident.

"Innovative and most daring" was likewise double-edged. To many of the heavy Captains, Arvada was the quintessential cavalry commander: dashing, impetuous, and doomed. Just the one you wanted on hand to lead a brilliant sacrificial charge. In the early stages of the war, with Naval Command's horizons were limited to finding the slowest way to lose, her lightning, dare-devil attacks inspired what had been a sagging spirit of resistance.

But her chosen strategy of probing deeper and deeper into the solarsphere of various stars struck many as replacing strategy and established data with a flip of the coin.

Brooks gave all this time to sink in.

"But even in times of war," he resumed, "not all, or even most, naval operations involve battle. General dispositions and strategy, logistics, shipboard discipline, and the thousand and one tasks attendant upon maintaining complex machinery in a demanding environment, these are the nuts and bolts of keeping our ships fit to fight. We already have a structure for dealing with that. Tried and proved not only by us over the years but by every successful naval force in history. It is called the chain of command.

"Consider this, all of you. If we accept Arvada Sattar, who is still when all is said and done a Lieutenant Commander of middling seniority, as the head of the fleet, what happens to that chain? Who, for instance, is second in command? Me? You? Some committee? Whoever feels like it at the time? If a battle group must be detached, what is the order of precedence? Do we ask Arvada Sattar to draw up a whole new order of command?"

Idiot. How could a man who'd seen battle be so petty-minded? Arvada wished someone else would make her case for her, and not force her to appear self-serving.

But that was the thing about swashbuckling your way to prominence. You became this semi-mythical figure, with your followers hanging behind to see what the oracle would pronounce.

"With the greatest respect, Admiral Brooks," she said from her metal-limbed wardroom chair, considerably less grand than his, "I have never proposed discarding the current chain of command. Nor would I think of claiming authority over every aspect of naval operations. What I seek is for my achievements to be acknowledged. And as a result, to be given as need arises command of a battle group. Such a force would be selected according to circumstances. I seek permanent command over nothing but my own ship."

Glancing around the screens, she saw most of the fast cruiser Captains nodding. Surprisingly, several of the heavy Captains, including Ayama Cleave, who she rather thought her supporter, and Solange O'Grady, who she definitely did not, nodded as well, though most of their counterparts sat tight-lipped and noncommittal.

She pressed on, dreadfully self-conscious. From her first days at the Academy, she'd had it drilled into her that junior officers were to be seen, not heard. To set off the sparkling brilliance of their superiors.

"As to what right I have to ask that you grant me such authority," she said, "I might point to our recent victory over the Collaborationists. I might also point to several victories that came before. Including the destruction of two Evolved line of battle ships. But while that should settle any questions as to either my underlying competence or my willingness to engage the enemy, that is not foremost in my claim."

There was some false modesty if ever there was some.

"What makes me unique among us is my knowledge of the Evolved. That knowledge has been hard-gained. And most difficult to convey. Impossible, in fact, unless you knew Sahan Kotori as I did."

Was that an argument in her favor? She saw Everson Brooks, ever the gentleman, lean forward with a predatory look. But she spoke the truth. There was no way to fine-tune a legend. You had to live it full-size, or be reduced to pretender.

"I also," she pointed out, "have taken an Evolved prisoner. Gradually he is yielding up valuable intelligence. Though not always realizing the fact."

"Surely," said Brooks, "if you have a prisoner, the disposition of such should be a matter for the whole fleet to decide."

"Again with respect, Admiral, I disagree. As I have been saying, I have a unique understanding of the Evolved."

"And are determined to keep it that way, apparently." Brooks shook his head at her obduracy. "Are you trying to use your prisoner as a bargaining chip? What if your superiors ordered you to turn him over to—" he stumbled, having nearly said Naval Command "—to the fleet at large? Would you accept the chain of command in that case?"

What, after you bastards handed the holobrain you insisted I turn over for "research" straight back to the Evolved?

"Admiral, I, along with many others whose faces you see here, battled fiercely to take the Evolved ship. We suffered terrible casualties."

"In an action you were not authorized to undertake."

She channeled her inner Sahan. "Authorized by who? Naval Command? The Citizens' Council? Those half of the fleet's Captains stuck on the beach after their ships were destroyed in drydock because they accepted the chain of command?"

She felt the heat rising in her voice, saw the enmity it engendered in some of the Captains. To hell with it. Let it ride.

"*I* destroyed two Evolved heavies. Not the chain of command. *I* took back the *Eustella.* I won our recent battle at Erigone because the Evolved reacted exactly how *I* predicted. *I* know how to fight this war. And I fully intend to do so."

Oh boy. Why not just shout "*stuff* the chain of command", whip Brooks the bird, and be done?

Give Brooks credit; he did not lose his temper, though a few of the other heavy Captains were clearly fuming.

"I think," he said with a show of calm, "that we can take that as a case in point. As tempers appear to be growing heated, let us put that question aside for the moment. I have one more item we need to address, then I will turn the discussion over to others."

He shuffled in his chair, then gave Arvada what she thought an oddly quizzical look. "There is one subject it seems to me we have been avoiding almost as much as who shall run the fleet. And that is, what is our relationship to be with the civilian population."

Uh-oh.

"Ever since the very beginning of the Evolved occupation," Brooks stated, "the Peregrines have been a people divided. Many took the enemy's side not out of conviction, but lack of choice. Following the battle of Demeter the Evolved, along with their quisling Raisa Catalan, established themselves in firm control of Harrar's Reach. Then began spreading out from there. For some time they appeared unstoppable. Now, thank God, the tide would appear to be turning."

Yes, Arvada thought darkly. Thanks to me and Sahan, though you'd never know to hear him tell it.

"For all the Evolved and Catalan in particular have suffered some bloody noses of late—"

The bloody noses *I* gave them.

"—yet the military situation remains unresolved. Meanwhile the Alliance is facing issues of its own. Naval Command still exists, formally—"

Junior officers did not normally make rude noises during an Admiral's presentation, but a chorus of vulgar suggestions showed what those present thought of Naval Command. Brooks laughed to show he was in on the joke.

"But I think we can all agree that Naval Command is a spent force. The Citizens' Council also suffered a major blow to its prestige when it collaborated with the Collaborationists in what was billed as 'peace talks,' only to end in the destruction of nearly half our fleet in drydock."

Another round of catcalls greeted mention of the Council.

"And yet," said Brooks, "the Citizens' Council remains the only body voted in by what was once called the Resistance. If they lose all authority, who then speaks for the Alliance? For our own citizens, wondering what life might look like after the war, what vision do we present?"

That at last brought silence to a meeting that since mention of Naval Command had been sinking toward your standard military bullshit session.

"We *need* the Citizens' Council," Brooks concluded. "That does not necessarily mean we go on allowing them a voice in military or strategic decisions. But we have to maintain the appearance — no, sorry, I misspoke, we have to maintain more than just the appearance — of democracy. We have to nurse and cultivate the thing itself. That is the Peregrine tradition.

And we must somehow assure the people that when this war is won, that tradition will still be holding strong."

No one had any argument to make. Arvada had one: how about we win the friggin' war first, or it will be someone else's decision. She held her peace, with difficulty.

With great solemnity Brooks nodded around at the faces of the other Captains he was seeing stacked along the walls of his own wardrobe. Everyone got two seconds of direct eye contact. The elder statesman.

"Of necessity, the military is going to assume an outsize role during and for some time after the war. But what is that role going to look like to the civilian population?"

He stared directly at Arvada. In silence, for a full five seconds.

"In particular, what would be the civilian perception of a fleet ruled by Arvada Sattar? Now like the rest of you, I know Captain Sattar. I know she honors the Peregrine tradition deep down in her blood, as her mother did before. So do not let anything I have to say in any way impugn Captain Sattar's personal ambitions."

Perish forfend. But Arvada knew some of them were thinking: her mother was a pushy bitch too.

"But to give a junior officer," Brooks was saying, "practical command of the fleet, whatever we call it, what tradition does that uphold? Or perhaps better to ask, what traditions does it not overthrow? That Arvada Sattar is the great hero of the war to date no one can deny. But that very title carries with it most dangerous undercurrents. For how far is military *hero* from *warlord*?"

Protests broke out among the fast cruiser Captains. Brooks spoke right over them. "This is not Captain Sattar's —

Arvada's, fault. It is but a simple fact of history that whenever some hero helps bring their country through a time of crisis, there are inevitably cries for them to continue in authority, to bring order to the disturbed times that always follow."

"If the Peregrine people love democracy as much as you say," shouted Wayland Takedi of the fast cruiser *Keyna*, "then they will not shout for some warlord to rule them. Nor will we give them one."

Brooks nodded patiently, despite the breach of protocol which must have his stomach fermenting acid. "I hope you are right. But once the very *idea* of a, say, claimant to the throne as it were, arises, history shows it can be a very hard thing to stamp out. Consider the original exodus of the *Stephen Hawking* from the tyranny and religious persecution of Earth at that time. And now think how once civilians come to believe that Arvada Sattar commands the fleet, whether literally true or not, how much unrest will it cause as new claimants arise simply because now the idea has been breached? How much unrest will result? At what point will freedom have to be curtailed in fact?"

"I am not asking to be placed in command of the fleet," Arvada interrupted. "Much less be proclaimed Queen or whatever you're suggesting with this 'claimant to the throne' bull— ah, rhetoric."

"All I'm saying," Brooks countered, though it clearly wasn't, "is that your name is associated with a special danger. Because it was you, Arvada Sattar, who initiated, on no authority but your own, the fatal strike against the *Elipida*. Yes, it damaged Evolved operations in Harrar's Reach. Though I doubt many of us here are clear exactly how. And we can expect even less comprehension among the civilian population. What everyone does understand is the number of civilian dead. Three thousand. Three thousand Peregrine civilians whose lives were lost in the break-up of the *Elipida*."

He paused to pat the air with his hands as claims and counter-claims filled the speaker. "Yes, yes, I know. Do they truly deserve civilian status when their work was devoted to the enemy navy? That has already become a subject of very hot debate both in the Alliance and within the Reach. That debate, I suggest, will make it more difficult to reunify the two populations. It will also more than likely serve as an issue for would-be demagogues on both sides of the issue. It will forever call into question a military apparently willing to sacrifice civilian lives to its own ends."

Now even some of the cruiser Captains were looking at each other across the screens, not wholly accepting of Everson Brooks' thesis, but not sure how to rebut it, either. Or even, to judge from some of the pained expressions Arvada saw, to know if they should.

"It would be much better for the Peregrine world," said Brooks, "if the entire issue could be forgotten. That, regrettably, is impossible. Here all we can do is ask ourselves, is it in the best interest of the peaceful, united people we all hope to see following the war, to raise Arvada Sattar's name to a position of such unavoidable prominence?"

Where was the deafening chorus rising to her defense?

Dead silence.

Arvada reached out, flicked off the screens.

Screw you all.

And yet....

Those three thousand deaths haunted her, too.

Chapter 24

Rows of images in precise squares were spread across the high wall of the training hall. Faces. Grinder faces. Images of the dead; maybe two hundred of them. Heavily backlit, so that in the funeral twilight of the hall fugitive motes of dust floated glinting before them, imparting an underwater effect.

Staring up at them stood rows of Grinders at a loose approximation of attention. Green fatigues hung limp on their narrow frames. Skeletal faces, living and dead, faced each other.

In the front row Sahan Kotori, staring back and forth, saw that while the Grinders assembled for the ceremony outnumbered those depicted on the wall, the same faces appeared on both sides.

The Grinders were clones.

Of course he'd known this. Even while still ... human? (He knew he had worn that form in one life as he wore this now, knew he'd been born to it, yet there appeared little to hold him there but bad memories. What defined the true narrative of his life?) While no Grinder brain had ever been taken intact by the Alliance, DNA samples gathered hurriedly from the dead confirmed that all derived from a set number of basic patterns, possibly as few as seventy or eighty.

Now he saw living and dead reflected in each other, as if in a mirror depicting the future.

An overburdened filtration system, not meant to handle as many Grinders as were currently crammed aboard the Evolved ship, left a scent of stale air salted with burned dust. The strict rationing of bathing facilities, also pressed past their original design, contributed a musty smell, plus that vague but distinctive fresh-meat scent of Grinders. Though grateful to find he could smell at all — the senses or lack thereof of this artificial body still sometimes puzzled him — he found the overall effect redolent of recent, gory death.

For some time silence reigned. Disquiet buzzed around inside his skull. He didn't know what role he was supposed to serve here. Ripples of energy stirred through his bloodstream. And something vaguely suggestive of the universal. He knew the Grinders — the other Grinders — felt the same.

Drugs. Inside him, that is. Drugs released by the holobrain. In the Grinders surrounding him the holobrain stimulated a release of hormones including some, Sahan guessed, not original to the form. The effects were so obviously artificial.

Images of the dead Grinders paraded across the wall and across his mind. Accompanying it came a dirge-like music he found rather dissonant; more martial than sentimental. Undoubtedly it too stirred the desired emotions in the Grinders.

He could stop neither the images nor the music. He could try to think around them, to realize that both were being transmitted directly to his mind by a holobrain. Bypassing what might otherwise be his own will.

The stream of images and music flowed on, and though he knew his own life stood outside it, Sahan could not avoid sharing some degree of the sensations that held the Grinders in thrall. Each of them saw the face, most often several times repeated, that was their own. Those apparent dead still lived — in them. Just as they would still live in those who followed.

Death was an illusion. You were but the immediate manifestation of a life that began long before your assigned quantum of awareness, and would survive longer still. What appeared to be death was merely the transition you underwent in the process of joining the larger whole.

Of immortality.

Lineaments of that grandeur seeped into Sahan's own awareness, though his rationality was not so overwhelmed he could not hold onto a well-honed skepticism. Still, the hormones coursing through his bloodstream could not be wholly denied.

At least none of these faces was his.

Fortunately. For he hated the idea of sharing any part of his life with anything else. His pain and his anger were his own.

Slowly everything changed. The faces of the dead began to blur and thin. Through them percolated scenes of the fighting that had claimed those glowing, ancestral visages.

Scenes taken unmistakably through sensor cameras revealed the dead's' last battle. Sahan saw Grinders crawling through wreckage, the area ahead of them murkily outlined in ghost-green and light gray. And when a suited Peregrine lurked ahead, a rusty dull infrared. The Grinders' sensors were inferior to those of the Peregrines. But serviceable enough for close-quarter battle.

And this was very close indeed. What the wreckage was Sahan didn't know. The stacked corridors leading past one room after another, their size difficult to gauge around collapsed roofs, bulging walls, and clouds of drifting dust, suggested a ship to him but it could also be the interface area of a Peregrine torus or possibly even a cylinder. If so, vacuum claimed it now.

The battleground was much too tight for rocket fire. Even flechettes offered only a hurried and uncertain shot at blobs of red wriggling like snakes through the dust and darkness. Most of the fighting was done with battle-saw, vibra-sword, and knife. Hands, rendered deadly by the powered suits, were frequently employed by the Peregrines. The Grinders responded with the mechanized teeth on their helmets.

He jerked, trying to roll away, as a white-suited figure launched itself at him from a thicket of broken wiring and twisted tubes dead ahead, no warning flash of infrared at all. The Peregrine fastened itself onto him, trying to bring a vibra-knife into play only to have it tangle in the debris. Sahan immediately engaged with his teeth. Since the Rigger's neck was protected by the suit's alloy locking ring he sank his churning jaws just below, trying to tear through to the trapezius and the subclavian artery deeper down.

The scene in his head shifted to another combat before he knew how the first turned out.

He fell exhausted to his knees as one brutal encounter after another engulfed him. He saw no Grinder in the hall still standing. He was gasping. Fear and rage crashed through him in great waves. But rage predominated. He threw himself with no thought of defense at blue-suited Marines and white-suited Riggers combing through the wreckage in overwhelming numbers.

Yet though his fury was real, it did not wholly take over his mind. A part of him still tried to analyze what was being done to him. A strand of rationality frayed and frightened, knowing through long habituation that to wander too far from the channels set for it brought PAIN.

Nevertheless that impulse of examination persevered, through habit and obstinacy.

These memories weren't his. He might have a Grinder body, but he'd never used it in combat.

The Evolved were controlling everything he saw. Or felt.

But he'd known that. Hadn't he?

When?

Certainly when he found himself in a Grinder body. But he must have known even before. From the very beginning. He had to. From his first memories following the moment when the Sun burnt out his eyes in one glorious moment of realization. From his first memories of—

PAIN!

Already rolling on the floor, he twisted onto his back, arching his spine and kicking down frantically with his heels. A Grinder rolled into him foaming and gyrating, knocking him onto his side.

PAIN!

He must have known. He must have.

PAIN!

Had his chest not been frozen tight he would have screamed.

Instead he retreated back into the scenes of hand-to-hand combat. Throwing himself at any flash of infrared or hint of blue or white. Twisting and grabbing and biting, just as the now-dead Grinders had done in their final moments.

He did not know it, but he had an erection.

Other Grinders were more aware. Scraps of green fluttered across the floor as fatigues were torn off. Frantically male and female Grinders sought each other in hammering copulation.

Still sharing the scenes in their heads, Sahan saw those of fury and destruction displaced by those of sex. This same sex taking place before him, right here and now.

With the images came associated sensations. He assumed they were hormone-induced. He didn't want them, but couldn't block them out. They bred not desire, but disgust.

For the Grinders, however, he sensed a sort of broad communion, a mixing of life and death, with the dead heroes on the wall wearing the same faces as the live Grinders copulating across the floor.

He would never be one of them.

Too disjointed by the flow or hormones to stand, he crawled to a corner of the room, past rolling and humping bodies like a vast battlefield of the fallen in their death-throes.

In the corner he curled up, hands about his knees. None approached him. He was Sahan Kotori, and a changeling. They partly feared, partly revered him.

He wanted only to pull away from this whole new nightmare that passed for his life.

How futile, when the Evolved had crawled right into his brain and lodged there.

***

"Now," Arvada told Beck, her Evolved prisoner, "you *will* tell me the truth. You will leave nothing out. You will hold nothing back because you think you might be able to play it to your advantage later."

Having decided it looked like a form of weakness to keep Beck in the brig, she'd assigned him his own quarters. Lord knows she'd lost enough people in taking his ship that there were plenty to spare. The room was cramped and bare and gray, Petty Officer Tapanni's belongings having all been stored away to bestow upon his relatives. Come the day the Alliance finally conquered Harrar's Reach, because that's where they were.

Of course the door was kept locked, the room monitored for any activity involving anything electrical, and Beck himself had two separate transponders, one in a silver ring around his wrist, the other subcutaneous. He complained to Arvada that all this amounted to petty harassment. She replied that she could easily change it to major if he chose.

He sat on the bed, slope-shouldered and bedraggled in the magenta fatigues he'd been supplied. His fingers and tight-pressed lips twitched. Periodically she could see the fatigues tighten over his shoulders as he clenched his stomach and tilted forward. Being isolated from the holobrain really was getting to him.

Let's see how much.

"I will say this one more time, purely for form's sake." His once-resonant baritone had climbed half an octave over the past several days, and thinned. "I demand — no, let's make that *request*, I can see demands don't sit well with you — to be turned over to your Naval Command or Citizens' Council." He looked up in apprehension. "*You* aren't Naval Command now, are you?"

"Think of me more like God." Arvada stood with her back to the door of Beck's quarters, trying to shut down memories of the room's last occupant because it might affect what little objectivity she had left. "I am sorry to keep making threats. It demeans us both. But I have questions for you regarding remarks you made about Sahan Kotori, and one way or another, I *will* have the truth."

Since the living Evolved had first suggested it, the possibility that Sahan might still be alive had eaten at her heart like an acid drip. If he held back now and she ended up killing him, that would make it easier to believe it was all a lie.

"You declared that Sahan did not in fact die at Harrar's Reach," she said. "That though badly injured, he was taken back to your homeworld to be ... reconstructed, was the word you used."

"This was what we were told."

"You further implied that if I could put you in contact with a holobrain, that you might be able to contact him in some way."

"I believe I said 'perhaps.' Or words to that effect. When and if he came back into Peregrine space."

"Please be very careful about your generalities. I am willing to allow a certain leeway for miscommunication. But if you are just blowing swamp gas in some attempt to manipulate me, tell me now. Or I *will* kill you. My name is Arvada Sattar, and this is my word on it."

Beck rolled his eyes at yet one more tiresome display of her primitive nature. It always surprised her how human he looked. Well he was, of course; they were both descendants of the Riggers who fled from Earth aboard the *Stephen Hawking*. The Evolved did not call themselves such for any great advancement of the human form or capabilities. It was the Group Mind — the dead, as Sahan called them, raising a sort of superstitious closet-lurking childhood fear — that embodied their "advances" and their capabilities.

"Again," he said, "purely for form's sake, killing me would violate every law of your people or mine."

"And just who *is* the law in your universe, Beck?"

"You are, Captain Sattar," he acknowledged, with a sardonic bow.

"Then formalities over, let us attend to the business at hand."

"I must say, I expected to see you before this."

"I was otherwise occupied." And afraid to face this question squarely. "Now do you stand by your statement that Sahan did not die at Harrar's Reach?"

"Again, that is what we were told. I have no direct knowledge."

"And just exactly what did you mean by 'reconstruction'?"

"I can only speculate. My impression was that extensive parts of his body had been damaged beyond repair and would have to be replaced. Likely all."

"Meaning?"

"He would emerge as a composite of organic and cybernetic materials. What you might call an android, except that it would all be powered by his own brain."

The inertial dampers tripled their pull, or so her weakening legs told her. She sagged back against the oval door.

This, this, this....

This isn't fair. We only so recently discovered the joys of each others' bodies, after so many years of denial!

To lose Sahan to death, that was war. It had destroyed any interest life held for her beyond vengeance, but she'd settled in to wear her pain like a shroud, and keep walking forward one step at a time.

To think of Sahan still alive, but his body, his flesh lost to her, that was monstrous. Some kind of existential mockery. If she believed any God/gods existed, she would curse them to their face.

And what if they laughed at you? You, who for so long built a wall around your heart and now come whining about the consequences?

"And his" — she paused for an extra breath, her heart having run aground in her tightening chest — "his mind?"

"What can I tell you? The Group Mind does not inform me of its plans unless it requires a living set of arms and legs to actualize them. The Master Holobrain could easily read every neural pathway still functioning in his brain. Would the information gained be significant? Normally, no. There is very little about any aspect of the Alliance we do not already know. In the case of Sahan Kotori, however, we face a different proposition. He is the only Peregrine ever to penetrate the holobrains." He paused. "With the possible exception of one other, likely mythical."

"Hypatia Wren?"

To her great satisfaction, Beck's eyes widened in surprise. "You know of her?"

Arvada almost told him that Sahan had met her. In the holobrain. That might have choked down his smugness some, but it might also expose Hypatia, if she truly still existed in the holobrain, to further danger.

"She became famous, or perhaps notorious is a better word, following the *Geniah* expedition."

"Yes, of course." He seemed relieved. Because if more than the myth he suggested, Hypatia Wren might pose some danger to the Evolved?

"Why are the Evolved keeping Sahan alive?" Arvada demanded. "Not just to torment him, surely." She remembered so clearly Sahan's fear coming out of the holobrain. If they'd preserved him just to torture him in such a visceral, endless way, she'd destroy every holobrain in the universe. Kill and go on killing even if the war should end.

"They would not do that," said Beck, easing her rage. "Even though he did do just that to one of ours. We are not so savage as you."

She almost asked if the Grinders were a product of Immaculate Conception. But first things first.

"You told me they do not inform you of their decisions."

"But I do know their *character*. After all, I will someday join them. My memories have been recorded in the Master Holobrain, ready to be reborn within the Group Mind."

"But they wouldn't do that with Sahan, would they?"

"To what end? Anyway, the very idea is impossible." Beck could not quite hide his revulsion at the idea of a lesser being such as Sahan Kotori sharing the same Valhalla he himself hoped to inhabit someday. "No matter how many memories are still accessible in his neural pathways, they are memories *past*. What goes to make a full ... *personality*, to use a crude approximation you might find accessible, is their living reaction to these events. Assembled over decades. For instance, with no holobrain available, any experiences I undergo aboard your ship are similarly lost to the Group Mind. The *memory* may survive, but it will be no more an inherent part of my personality, or any other within the Group Mind, than if I'd read an account of someone else's adventures. It will in no way be experiential. However, I have already built up a broad library of recorded experiences. Sahan Kotori's would only begin when" — he glanced at her uneasily — "he is brought to some form of consciousness."

Arvada soothed herself with the image of pulling off Beck's fingers one by one. Recovered, she came back to the topic.

"So if they are not going to punish him, or incorporate him into the Group Mind, then what? Why pull him back from the edge of death?"

He shook his head at her obtuseness. "Can't you see?"

"Tell me."

"To use as a weapon."

"A weapon?"

"Against you, Captain Sattar. Against you."

Chapter 25

As Sahan huddled in his corner, the orgy taking place before him amid a heaving green mat of Grinders slowly wore down as the hormones coursing through them could no longer make up for the energy spent. The images of copulation being fed to their minds by the holobrains faded and died. Soon only exhaustion remained.

And shame.

For as if wakening from a dream, the Grinders now sprawled along the floor of the training hall groped frantically for any fragments of clothes to cover their nakedness. Most of their fatigues had already been ripped to shreds at the commencement of the orgy. What remained underwent a similar fate as squabbles broke out, blows were struck, and protuberant teeth snapped down on flesh as two or sometimes three Grinders would grab at the same green garment.

Finally, clad as best they could in the ripped and frequently blood-stained fatigues, the Grinders did try to get back on their feet, but drew as far apart from each other as space allowed, keeping their eyes fixed on the floor.

Sahan did not understand why a people who would literally chew you to pieces, people who so far as he knew lived a wholly shared military existence with no compunctions at all about nudity, would now be so shy over the sight of flesh, or even at having pitched in to what amounted to an all-hands-on-deck orgy.

But he was about to. Because a new series of images came to him.

Images whose source he was this time careful not to question.

Images of human beings.

But strangely dressed, to his eyes. Their clothing was archaic. Earth-like, but from a long-gone era even so. Their garments, baggy, dirt-stained shirts and ... trousers? — did not appear to be of any plasticene. He knew other materials had reigned for centuries. Wool, that was from sheep. Silk, from worms. Linen, from ... something. Wheat?

The images, the people, had emerged against an empty backdrop. Now their surroundings began to fill in.

Sahan's mind reeled.

Farmers! He'd know them anywhere. The Dainichi, his adopted people, regarded themselves primarily as farmers, though in truth their activities were far more widespread.

But even the Dainichi wore clothes of plasticene, that didn't wear out every two days and take massive amounts of water and cleansers to work in among the coarse fibers. And while the Dainichi retained much hand cultivation, they did not shun machinery for the heavier or more odious tasks. Nor did they keep large animals. Why would they? They didn't eat meat anyway, and if they ever did, cultured tissue imposed a much lower resource imprint upon a sealed habitat.

These hearty, smiling farmers he saw inside his skull stood amid cows, horses, sheep, pigs, ducks. Fields, some green, some the brown of fresh-tilled soil —Earth? — stretched off in every direction, under a blue sky so benevolent the few clouds seemed added just to lend it character.

Where? Walls of even the largest cylinders would be seen rising to either side, and stretch fore and aft either to distant end caps or sector seals. Here, the horizon fell off on all sides. Sahan had stood on planets, though none where you'd care to take your helmet off, and noted similar horizons. Disorienting, to live on a surface where everything curved down, and the rotation wasn't there to hold you *to* the ground, but spin you off.

Earth, then. With happy people gathering together in fellowship before archaic buildings he knew from his studies of history to be made of wood and glass, fragile and fire-prone as they might be.

He knew everyone was happy because besides their smiles and frequent hugs, that's how he now felt himself.

Sort of. Examining the impression more closely, he found himself not so much truly happy as perked-up. Pulsing with energy, eager to deploy his body. Which in his case generally meant fighting.

The Grinders, contemplating the prosperous farmers and their infinity of space, as contrasted with the close, primitive quarters of shipboard life, immediately contrasted them with their own debased state. Which led quite literally to much groaning and gnashing of sturdy teeth.

They *know* these people, thought Sahan.

Only they couldn't turn away, because the images, which Sahan knew must be transmitted by holobrain, were inside their own heads. Many, male and female both, wept copiously. Sahan had never imagined Grinders doing that.

Then with scant transition, all was chaos and terror. Giant vehicles with huge, black, deeply grooved wheels, of the sort seen on the surface of mining colonies, came lumbering forward. Crushing crops, animals, buildings, and farmers, who fleeing this way and that from the monsters, jammed together too tightly to escape. The grooves in the wheels soon sprayed red blood across the green fields.

Other humans jumped down from the vehicles. Dressed in tight-fitting blue suits, they swung clubs left and right. Men, women, children, all were knocked senseless amid their own fields, now reduced to a wasteland of dark, churned-up Earth. The great black wheels rolled remorselessly over the fallen.

Fear, disgust, and hatred burned in Sahan's veins. Though some of the cause must be chemical, his own natural feelings, such as were left to him, were affronted by this scene of massacre.

In moments the whole population of farmers lay still or feebly crawling. Many were squashed to a pulp.

If only it had stopped there.

But now the true horror began. For the invaders began dragging the fallen farmers, men, women, and children, by their heels. Now it turned out that they were not dead after all. Even those squashed beyond recognition somehow regained human form.

From nowhere long scaffolds arose. The victims screamed and pleaded for mercy, kneeling with hands folded before them. But no mercy was to be had. One by one the farmers, of all sexes and ages, were strung up by their heels.

Screams of rage came from the Grinders.

The attackers ripped the clothes off the hanging people, leaving them naked. Then they—

Now it was Sahan's turn to try to turn away. He couldn't. He pressed his hands over his eyes, but the images still flowed inside his head.

So he watched helpless as the aggressors began skinning their victims alive. Wielding hooked knives, they stripped the flesh off the screaming people.

Sahan smashed a fist against his own head, trying to knock the images out.

Yet one more surprise. As the farmers' flesh was ripped away, what was revealed beneath wasn't raw and bloody flesh. The victims *looked* skinned, true, with all muscles exposed to view.

But the tissue thus revealed was green, with streaks of yellow running through. And the faces, instead of bleeding as the flesh was torn away, elongated and developed enormous teeth, as well as oversized, vertically oriented eyes.

Grinders.

Still it was not over. The Grinder bodies hanging by their heels were cut down and loaded onto the great trucks, the aggressors laughing at the nakedness of their deformed bodies.

Next the bodies, weakly struggling, were tossed down from the trucks. Which had somehow boarded a spacecraft. Because Riggers in white space suits carried the bodies into vast airlocks. From which they were expelled screaming — very briefly — into space.

Recovering, slowly, from his horror, his heart still pounding, Sahan realized he had just witnessed the Grinder creation myth.

The farmers he saw were a highly idealized vision of the Christian colony aboard the *Stephen Hawking*. So idealized that the curved walls of the habitat lay flat to imitate Earth. Nor would any habitat, then or now, include such extensive swaths of plowed earth, let alone herds of cows, sheep, and pigs.

His own knowledge of Christianity was spotty. But this was no exercise in abstract religious metaphor. Though the Grinders no doubt experienced the whole scene more viscerally, his own mind furnished cues.

This was the expulsion from ... his mind reached, settled on *Paradise.*

He ran through his small knowledge of expulsion myths from Earth. All falls from paradise, he'd learned somewhere, involved some offense. Some *sin.*

What sin had the farmers been guilty of?

Again the answer came from within his own head, but without thought. Instead, he shared the thoughts of the Grinders cowering away from the vision.

They'd let the other humans — the "bad angels," did he have that right? — carry them too far from Earth. They should have fought. Instead they tended to their gardens and their prayers, all the time moving further and further away from God's realm, and His protection.

They'd left their God behind.

Now he could no longer protect them. And they all bore witness to the consequences.

God did not exist in Grinder form. In being stripped of their humanity, the Grinders had been stripped of their God. That the (demons-devils-bad angels-infidels) were now the ones to go about clad in God's form remained the living symbol of their shame, which was revealed anew each time they stood naked.

Though sexual urgency could drive them to shed that taboo, the very act shamed them further. Because sex could not result in procreation. That glorification of God, that making that reflected the great Maker, was for them no more than a hollow mockery.

God did not exist in space. He did not exist in the Peregrine colonies.

He existed only in the heavens surrounding Earth. And if they were ever to be redeemed, if ever they would regain their human form, that must be the scene of the final battle.

Sahan groped to interpret this, mixing memory of the basic religious ideologies the Dainichi had been scrupulous to impart, with the images imparted by the holobrain, and the emotions more or less overflowing from the Grinders.

Inevitably he thought of his own casting-out by Arvada.

PAIN!

The Grinders ceased their self-recriminations to watch this strange creature fall and beat his body against the floor, screaming.

It seemed to them, in a vague, inarticulate sort of way, that this creature, who had in his own life retraced the trajectory that created their race, was taking on himself the collective guilt they all huddled away from.

***

"THEY WOULD USE *SAHAN* against me?" Arvada repeated incredulously. Beck's assertion did not compute.

No one could turn Sahan against her. Since they were teenagers at the Academy his loyalty had been the one unassailable certainty in her life. Friends might turn jealous and spiteful. Mothers might decide the further you wandered from their prescribed course the more you resembled a wretched infidel. Lovers who swore eternal passion one day might develop wandering eyes the next.

But no matter how he might bristle and bluster, never had Arvada known one moment when she did not believe Sahan Kotori would lay down his life for her on the instant. Including before *and* after their star-crossed on-again off-again love affair at the Academy.

"If you're trying to trick me," she told Beck, "you damn well better succeed. And I don't think you're good enough."

He slumped lower on the bed, hugging his arms about himself as shivers broke out. "Call it wishful thinking, then."

"You are entering on *very* dangerous ground."

He whirled, slamming the bottom of his fist into the wall behind him. The gesture was so fast she reevaluated her opinion that she could take him hand-to-hand.

"Dangerous?" he shouted. "Captain, you're *torturing* me!"

Well yes, she supposed she was. Fairly deliberately, too. Of course she had her reasons. But when Arvada looked at herself in the light of this enemy's sufferings, she winced at the callousness she saw.

Stepping forward, she sat at the foot of the bed, well within arm's reach. The slick blue sheet, designed to achieve optimum temperature for the body it covered and need no maintenance beyond an occasional pass through the sonic bath, had finger marks pressed into it. That was impossible.

"Tell me about it," she said.

"So you can gloat?"

"Tell me or don't." She started to rise.

He held up his hand.

"Loneliness, Captain. Loneliness of a dimension you cannot possibly imagine — and I recognize you have suffered a severe loss of your own. For which, I am sorry. Not for the man you mourn for. But the pain you bear, that I regret."

"Thank you."

"But do you feel completely cut off from all other life? Do you feel like the one single mote of dust in a universe of vacuum? Are you plagued with the sensation of falling away on all sides, always *falling*? You are heartbroken, Captain Sattar. But are you terrified? I am. With such a terror that must shortly drive me mad. And eventually kill me. Do you believe me?"

"Yes, I do," she said, recalling Sahan's descriptions of the Terror Barrier. And his sweat, his shivering, his restless shifting that never brought him to a place he could settle. And that was Sahan, too proud to acknowledge either pain or fear. "I do know a little of these things."

"And you can still stand there and watch me suffer with utter indifference?"

"Not quite utter."

A thin laugh trickled from his throat. "My condition must be severe indeed, to render me susceptible to Peregrine humor." He worked himself erect from his slumped posture, no more than a slight twitch in his fingers and at the corners of his mouth indicating his distress.

"Can I tempt you with a paradox, Captain? Your people are born, and die, and live all your lives separate from one another. Totally self-contained biological units. You cannot truly share emotions, not even during sex. To communicate your ideas you strip them of half their meaning. We — my kind — look at you, and recoil from what we see as soul-crushing isolation."

"Horrifying you is some satisfaction, I suppose."

"But in truth, your loneliness is shallow. Because you have never been truly *one*."

"And you have?"

"Not completely, no. The total mind-and-soul merging of an entire community that characterizes the Group Mind, that is still beyond me. And will be so long as I exist in this realm, outside the Master Holobrain. But through its medium, I have shared a sense of *being* with my people, both those living workers like myself, and with the Group Mind, which occupies a higher dimension."

"Death, you mean?"

"I mean a state I cannot describe and you cannot comprehend. A mutual awareness that dissolves the boundaries of individual existence. That sensation, though in a more generalized fashion, more of a ... mood, to employ a simplification you might understand, can be extended through the subordinate holobrains."

"And now," she said, "you are thrown onto your own resources. And finding them sadly lacking."

"I had hoped, though I can't think why, for a higher level of empathy from you, Captain Sattar. You are exceptional among your people. A great battle leader. Such appear from time to time. Wholly unpredictable. An affront to rational planning. But in the quality of your soul, there you are boringly pedestrian."

That hurt. She'd been thinking much the same thing since Sahan's death. For all her reputation for breaking with convention, it had been nothing but a most conventional concern for her career that made her keep Sahan at arm's length during her rise to command and after.

Beck's hands, which he'd been holding rigidly against his thighs to clamp down on the twitching, found the sheets. Gathering up a broad swath of fabric, his fingers began to work industrially in a way Arvada knew would exhaust her own hands in minutes.

"Sahan Kotori too violated all rational expectations. Had we known such a penetration of the holobrain was possible to your people, we might have sought harder for counter-measures before entering into this war. Perhaps we — the Evolved — would have put more effort into negotiations."

"Like any at all?"

He ignored that. "Your people, and Earth behind them, are expanding too fast. Your technology is too destructive, your methods to regulate it no more advanced than those of the Greeks and Trojans. How long, how far, were we supposed to run? But perhaps we fixated too much on the same old legends."

"Legends?"

"How the *Stephen Hawking* was forced to flee to the stars despite being wholly inadequate to the challenges it must face. Of the martyrdom of Beck Egan, for whom I am named. How our survival depended on solving hosts of problems beyond the science of the time. A leap of faith, in the most literal sense. How your continued expansion has forced us to keep fleeing, so that we must restrict our civilization to artificial habitats, forgoing any chance to feel ground beneath our feet and see sky above. Surely that much was our birthright?"

"And the Christians, what was their birthright? Or should I say, the Grinders?"

He flinched. "Ah. Yes. Them. We knew there must be a reckoning for that."

"Since you find me such a heartless savage, I'm interested to hear the highly evolved morality that led you to turn human beings into ... bug-eyed monsters."

"The Christians were forced on us when we were still at L5! Earth intended to replace the Riggers with Christians. As if that could ever work. Then they could follow through on their threat to excise the implants from our brains because they were not in the image of God. Given the technology of the time, we would have emerged, if at all, at a lower intellectual level than the Grinders.

"*That* was why we were forced to flee L5 long before the *Hawking* was anything like ready. But of course you know all this. It's your heritage same as ours. What you appear to have glossed over, however, is how the Christians remained a negative force for years. A constant threat. They refused to learn science, refused birth control until told the alternative was no births at all. Insisted on a resource-intensive way of life that in such a closed environment could not be sustained. And finally they demanded that we — the Riggers of the *Hawking*, your ancestors and mine — turn the ship around and return to Earth. To Earth! When their demand was refused, they staged a revolt. Swore they'd rather destroy the whole cylinder than go any further, because in death they would return to God. How can you deal with such people? They burned food stores. Can you imagine? Massive fires in a habitat already on the knife-edge of survival? Not to mention imminent starvation and roving mobs. They had to be stopped."

"By turning them into Grinders."

"That came later. We knew Earth would never stop pursuing us until they 'rescued' the Christian colony they'd forced upon us in the first place. We knew how they must react to our efforts to save ourselves. It had to come to war eventually. Not only was our population far too small to field soldiers in our defense, we … well, immortality in a state of transcendent joy is not something so easily surrendered as a mere individual life. So we turned to the only resource at hand."

He waved a hand at the close gray walls of a dead man's room. "And now we all must suffer for it. You and I both, Captain Sattar. Your people and mine."

In that moment Arvada felt an unexpected twinge of fellow-feeling. She almost felt sorry for the suffering he'd endured. Yet she doubted he'd be so forthcoming without it.

"Tell me again about Sahan. Making him into a weapon against me, I mean."

"Isn't it obvious? Obsession has two sides. Hate and love might express themselves in opposite ways. But inside the brain? They are no more than bundles of neural pathways. Change the routing, and all the passion directed toward one can easily be diverted to the other."

In a moment all her vain assurance that Sahan could never be turned against her was torn away.

And if Sahan *did* start hunting her … the thought was too frightening to follow out.

And yet….

Beck told her that given a holobrain, he might be able to reach Sahan. She resisted asking him exactly what that meant. Maybe he himself didn't know for sure.

Maybe he'd find some way to use it against her.

She had to chance it. She *must* find a way to reach Sahan. No matter what the Evolved thought they'd made of him, Arvada was sure that could the two of them just … communicate, she could revive the love in him.

"I think I understand the danger you face," she told Beck. "I am not such a savage as to want to see you fall into the Terror Barrier. And yet, to procure a holobrain, that is no easy thing. By their very nature they come surrounded by Evolved ships or hordes of Grinders."

"You *could* turn me over to your Citizens' Council."

"The same Citizens' Council that lost half our navy at the *Kepler* then declared me a war criminal? You do not help your position any with talk of the Citizens' Council. Your fate is in my hands. Get used to it."

Beck groaned.

"I might," she said, "out of the goodness of my heart, try to get you a holobrain. But to undertake such a risk, I would obviously require something in return."

He glanced at her suspiciously. "What, exactly?"

"Do I take it that 'exactly' means you aren't interested after all?"

"No!" He gasped for air. "No," he repeated more calmly. "But I can't possibly swear to such an open-ended proposition."

"Well that is your choice, of course. Pity. I really will get a twinge of guilt from time to time, thinking of you in the Terror Barrier. I'm not quite the savage you think I am." She saw him flinch. "And I will miss our little conversations."

She started for the door.

"Captain Sattar!"

She turned.

"This is unconscionable."

"Is that a yes, or a no?"

"By what right—"

"Yes, or no?"

A shrug tight enough to bulge muscles all along his neck and jaw lifted his shoulders nearly to his ears.

"If you can in fact procure a holobrain ... I promise I will do my best to meet your demands. Because I know full well what will happen if I don't."

"See?" she said, beaming. "Communication between our races *is* possible. So why don't we regard this as a first step on the long road to peace?"

"Because it's not. It is you employing shameful and illicit means to gain an advantage a prisoner wholly at your mercy. Peace is your worst nightmare."

Touché.

Walking up the corridor, Arvada knew this was a bad idea.

Or would have been, had there not been Sahan to reckon with.

She had more than her heart on the line, though in truth that remained uppermost in her thoughts.

Sahan was just too dangerous. She *must* try and turn him from any imagined vengeance.

Because as he'd proved time and again in the Decahedron, he could read her a lot quicker than she could read him.

Chapter 26

Once more into the sun.

To Arvada Sattar, belted in the Captain's chair of the *Geirovar*, it seemed she'd spent half the war lurking in various solarspheres. Keeping an anxious eye on the monitors, stomach churning while she assured Engineering she had the situation well in hand.

Here, though, she could leave the monitors to others. The screens curving across the front of the bridge had been integrated into one grand image. A yellow mass shooting off occasional sparks and twisting flames filled the lower half. But above that could be seen the deep dark blue of space, with a shimmering sea of stars across the top.

By Arvada's standards, the Alliance fleet barely skimmed the star.

They were still deep enough that along with other measures such as spreading chaff and shimmering their hulls' outlines, the radiation should shield them from the enemy fleet.

Though suited up for battle, the people moved about the bridge with that slightly lagging underwater rhythm typically imparted by the inertial dampers. With their helmets hooked close by but not clapped on, Arvada saw far more anticipation than worry. Even smiles.

She smiled herself, basking in the comfort of going into battle with such veterans. So different from the first days of the war, when they all, most especially her and Sahan, had to make it up as they went along. Now even the newest hands, having survived the roller-coaster plunge into the sun after the Collaborationist heavy *Filia*, were confident that no matter how frightened they felt, they would do their jobs and trust their Captain to do hers. Which was to get them through.

Arvada hoped the same air of relaxed readiness prevailed aboard the other ships. Few of them had the same experience of lurking deep in the solarsphere her people did. Though it was spreading fast.

The fleet consisted of ten fast cruisers and four heavies, in orbit about the upper reaches of the star Rione. Six planets circled the sun, of which only the distant orange-gray gas giant was visible under current magnification. Two of the six offered a breathable atmosphere — for eight to ten minutes. One other, the nitric-acid circulating Mearr, would kill you within a few excruciating seconds.

But the second planet out, red-streaked Flanna, on the border of an asteroid belt, hosted one of the richest mining colonies in Peregrine space. And to keep the Peregrine miners at their tasks, one of the largest concentration of Grinder troops in any of the occupied habitats had been stationed there.

And where there were Grinders, there would be a holobrain.

Though that was not her ostensible purpose here. She'd assured the Captains assembled in war council that the Collaborationist fleet would make an excursion from Harrar's Reach to recover Grinders from outlying colonies they could no longer defend.

Staked her reputation on it, in fact. And whatever slender hold on authority she might possess.

She'd sweated it for a while, too, keeping the task force positioned to swoop down on whichever of three locations Arvada had predicted the evacuation would come. First she'd had to wait several days for the scout drones to report activity. While questioning — check that; outright grousing — among the other commanders, at least half of them senior to her, mounted toward outright challenge.

Then at last the drones hidden in the solarsphere of Rione reported the arrival of a Collaborationist fleet.

Next came the scramble to execute the three Jumps that would take them here. At a depth that would hide them from enemy drones still doing battle with their Alliance counterparts stationed around any sun hosting a colony still held by the Evolved. Had they arrived too late, that too would have put big dents in Arvada's authority. Which rested on nothing but legend.

But the enemy fleet had to make the journey out to the colony at Flanna, embark the Grinders, and return.

The screens, though muddled by radiation at this level, showed them cruising at fleet speed toward Rione, fat, dumb, and happy.

Far as Arvada was concerned, the hard part had been accomplished. Now all she had to do was win the battle.

***

"Why am I having such a sensation of deja vu?" Admiral Brooks asked rhetorically. "Here we have another proposal from Arvada Sattar, and I find myself wondering, am I looking at an actionable plan of battle? A metaphysical tract? A satire? The whole concoction appears conjured up, and I use the word advisedly, out of equal parts pseudo-mystical speculation and sheer self-acknowledged guesswork. All based on unverifiable 'intelligence'" — his fingers traced quotation marks in the air — "from an enemy prisoner who has no reason to wish us well."

Arvada leaned back with apparent relaxation, much forced, in the wardroom of the *Geirovar*. The other fleet Captains looked down on her from the wall screens, their expressions ranging from scornful to thoughtful to, among some of the cruiser commanders, eager.

A cup of coffee, from which she reminded herself occasionally to take casual sips, steamed before her, reflecting her mood, if not her countenance. Brooks' opening summation followed the exact line she'd expected.

His weary visage occupied the center screen.

"Why," he asked Arvada, "would your prisoner, this Evolved who calls himself Beck, provide us with authentic information?"

A delicate question.

"The living Evolved," she said, "are very subject to loneliness. More than we can truly comprehend. The need for communication runs very high in them." Especially when they're shaking themselves to pieces.

"Loneliness? He has turned turned spy because he's *lonely*? Your powers of persuasion must be considerable, Captain Sattar."

He paused to let the implications sink in, hoping for sniggers. And got one or two from some senior Captains. Everyone else ignored the barb, wanting to get down to business. Arvada's plan might appear far-fetched, but no one had any other. And she'd made dreams come true before now.

"If we are to rely on information from this prisoner of yours," Brooks said, "at the least he should be made available to the Fleet. Not kept to yourself like a private crystal ball." He smiled, pleased with the analogy.

"With respect, Admiral," she said, "I believe that previous experience makes me best suited to interrogate the prisoner."

"Obviously. Just as you have repeatedly believed that neither the chain of command nor the collective wisdom of our fellow Captains gathered here were worthy of consideration."

"Again with respect, I am not clear as to your meaning. I am setting forth the information I have gathered for consideration before all Captains actively engaged in resistance to the Evolved. I would also point out that regarding the Evolved, I have on several occasions provided information that proved accurate, and resulted in victories. As for ignoring the chain of command, if any of us here truly adhered to that, their ships would lie wrecked in drydock along with those of other Captains who believed the directives of Naval Command could never be questioned. All through this war the chain of command as been a moving target."

This was more than skirting insubordination; more like jumping in with both feet. What the hell. Might as well be hung for a lamb as a ... whatever. Arvada braced for a public spanking.

But Everson Brooks only spread his hands wide, sinking back in his chair in a resigned gesture. "And that is the frustrating thing."

He wore fatigues instead of the full dress uniform with its stacked rows of ribbons she'd expected. The strain of command had lowered the shades over his once piercing blue eyes.

Ayama Cleaves, John Two-Vests, and Solange O'Grady all sat stone-faced, their attention fixed on him, but far from reverential. Arvada wondered if the Admiral had received an off the record talking-to from some of the heavy Captains anxious that the fleet not revert to the bad old days of the "fleet in being."

"You have been reckless, ruthless, and insubordinate," Brooks told her, yet without much steel in his voice. "You are, in fact, a declared war criminal. Personally I question why we do not relieve you of command and place you under arrest."

He shook his head disgustedly. While Cleaves, John Two-Vests, and O'Grady only intensified their poker stares.

"And *yet*," said Brooks, in a more composed tone. "That is what I keep hearing. And *yet*. And yet you admittedly have scored victories, including the destruction of two Evolved heavies. And you have made yourself a hero of the people, for all the controversy still surrounding the deaths aboard the *Elipida*."

He glared at her accusingly, as if it was her fault for winning battles in such unconventional ways. "And so we are forced to seriously weigh this latest proposal of yours, bizarre as it appears."

"Thank you, sir."

Brooks grunted to show what he thought of her thanks. He made a show of considering the console before him, saving him from looking at her. "You say the Evolved will restrict their heavies to Harrar's Reach because the ... *living* Evolved?" He held up his hand. "No, don't explain. Because the Evolved there don't dare put their lives to the slightest risk. Not without something called a 'Master Holobrain.' Which, one presumes, is a central holobrain in command of all the others."

"If I may, sir, it is also the repository of the Group Mind."

"Ah yes, the Group Mind. We'll just take that as given, shall we? Apparently the original Master Holobrain was destroyed by Sahan Kotori in his attack on the *Elipida*. The less said about that the better. But now you're saying the Evolved heavies will no longer sail from Harrar's Reach."

"Not if there is any chance they will encounter combat. Not until a new Master Holobrain is brought into the system. Sir."

"Your informant, this Beck, claims that due to recent reverses suffered by the enemy, and in particular heavy losses to the Collaborationist fleet" — he did not mention just who was responsible for that — "the enemy plans to pull Grinder infantry now occupying the outlying colonies back to Harrar's Reach. It appears they have limited numbers of Grinder troops available — that's a relief, if true — and no longer feel able to support outposts beyond the Reach. If correct, the enemy would appear to be strengthening their defenses in the Reach itself."

"That is what Beck believes, Admiral. Though the evacuation of the Grinders is likely meant not so much for defense as to preserve them for further operations, should the opportunity arise. That is, should the arrival of a new Master Holobrain once more make offensive operations possible. The number of Grinders available to the Evolved even in the homeworld is limited. Like any slave society, they fear their own slaves, so they kept their numbers limited. And though the Grinders are clones, and can be produced quickly, they still cannot be raised and trained within the framework now available. In all, the Evolved may have no more than two thousand Grinders left to them, including those in Peregrine space. I can't verify that number, but I believe it a sound working hypothesis."

"Your prisoner seems remarkably cooperative." Brooks' brows wrinkled as he hovered on the verge of asking why. Then eased as he realized he did not want to know what means a declared war criminal might have used to obtain such intelligence.

"I believe, Sir," said Arvada, "that we have an opportunity here to deliver a blow to the Collaborationist fleet."

Another confused interchange broke out among the screens, but died as Red-headed, freckled, square-jawed Solange O'Grady took over the conversation.

"With permission?" she asked Brook, who as senior officer had been serving as chair. He waved his assent almost absently.

Arvada braced for whatever might come. She'd entered into battle alongside Solange O'Grady on several occasions, and knew the woman was far from shy when it came to denting tin. On the other hand, O'Grady was much her senior, and their aggressiveness, though leading to mutual respect, also engendered a competitive element.

"Captain Sattar," said O'Grady. "You tell us that the Evolved prisoner Beck revealed to you that the first station the Evolved meant to visit was Chitra. That being one of the closest in, and with probably the largest garrison of Grinder troops."

"Yes, Sir."

"But it is now your opinion that since the failure of Beck's mission, the destination will be changed. Because they will presume Beck has informed you of the plan."

"That is correct, Captain."

"That still leaves several other possible sites. So your plan is to station the task force where it will have a chance to engage at three different colonies. Yet to me it appears you have picked the mining colony Flanna as the most readily accessible. To the extent that the chance of reaching some of the further systems before Catalan's ships evacuate the Grinders and make their Jump back to the Reach becomes, in my opinion, marginal at best."

"Yes, Captain O'Grady. I believe that without Evolved support the Collaborationists will go no further than they absolutely have to. That conclusion is based in part of my assessment of their morale. The further out they go, the more they risk the chance not just of interception, but of mutiny. By that standard, Flanna strikes me as the most likely target. Though we still have at least some chance to trap her fleet if they visit any of the other systems."

"Very stirring, as always, Captain Sattar," said Solange O'Grady, but despite the sarcasm inherent in her words they did not come across as demeaning. "One final question before I turn the chair back over to Admiral Brooks. Some of us are concerned about a possible attack on the *Kepler*, which at the moment is the Peregrine seat of government. You don't believe that likely?"

An embarrassed silence fell over the room. Clearly the strategy to keep the fleet in position to defend the *Kepler* was favored by Admiral Brooks. Equally clearly, to Solange O'Grady and many others, such a plan was unacceptably passive.

"I do not believe it likely at this time, Captain O'Grady. Not without Evolved support."

"Which you are convinced will not occur."

"Not in the near future. Sir."

"Thank you, Captain Sattar." She swept her eyes around the screens. "Of course my vote counts for no more than anyone else's at this council. But it appears to me that the plan to position a task force to attack the enemy fleet at Flanna, as well as some other locations, seems sound. As for leaving the *Kepler* with reduced defenses, the feasibility of that depends on just what we make of Captain Sattar's assertion that the Evolved will not stir from Harrar's Reach. At least in the near term."

She let that sink in for a moment.

"Like all of you," Solange O'Grady continued, "I have at times found myself questioning some of Arvada Sattar's tactics. Because I did not understand the reasons behind them. Like many of you, I questioned both her and Sahan Kotori. Nor do I understand all of what Captain Sattar tells us even now. But I think the time has come to acknowledge this much. Following Demeter I, like all of you, resisted capitulation. But I had no idea of how to fight the Evolved. And to my shame, little hope.

"Now everything is changed. Why? Because of Arvada Sattar. It truly is that simple. Let us acknowledge it. However, I have overstayed my invitation. Captain Brooks, if you would resume the chair?"

Brooks just sat leaning forward over spread elbows, looking slightly dazed as he realized that not only his authority, but his time, had passed.

Then, unexpectedly, he laughed. Or rather, coughed with an edge of attempted humor riding it.

"Things were done differently, when I was a Lieutenant Commander." He shook his head sadly in nostalgia for times gone by, when Peregrine officers did not battle enemies in holobrains, and strategize around something called the Terror Barrier. With visible effort he pulled himself together, straightening in his chair.

"Once again Arvada Sattar has come telling her elders of mysteries and wonders. And we listen spellbound, and bid her take the defense of the Alliance from our hands."

He chuckled to himself, eyes averted from the screens. "Nine, maybe ten years ago it would have been, I watched the Alliance Championships for the Decahedron. When a young Academy cadet, a Dainichi we were told, reached the finals, I was incredulous. A Dainichi? But they're pacifists! And the other four finalists were all professionals, veterans of many bouts. How he even got so far was a mystery. And then I watched that Dainichi, a scrawny-looking fellow by the name of Sahan Kotori, pulverize all four, one after the other."

He shook his head at the irony of it all. "I did not know at the time I was watching the future. Now if you all will excuse me, I have much work to do seeing to repairs on the *Argo*. Captain O'Grady, would you oblige me by a taking the chair?"

And that was how Arvada Sattar took command of a task force entering into battle against the Collaborationists.

Chapter 27

Arvada was growing tired of the same vertical triptych stretched across the bridge screen: flickering red-yellow arrows of solar eruptions shooting up from the bottom, a barren stretch in the middle of shimmering darkness, and the fringe of stars dancing along the top, waving in rhythm to the stronger eruptions of flame.

Ten times an hour she suppressed the urge to ask Tarika Okada, supervising the row of scanner consoles at the front of the bridge, if the enemy fleet was getting any goddamn closer, or going in circles.

Distant as they were from the star's core, such a long accumulation of heat was beginning to put a strain on the cooling and recycling systems, imparting that particular scent of heated metal doused with cleaning fluid that roused instinctual fears in those trapped in a closed environment. The suits the crew all wore, though normally little strain to move in, were turning bloated and irritating as they were maneuvered around the confines of the bridge.

The easy-going atmosphere that had prevailed when the *Geirovar*, along with the rest of the task force, took station to set an ambush in the solarsphere of Rione had long since turned that a mix of fierce boredom and gnawing anxiety that strikes even veteran troops who have to wait too long for battle.

The left arm of her chair squealed in protest. The power enhancement on the suits worn by the crew had been switched off. But somehow her left hand, working nervously, had re-engaged that separately controlled section, then squeezed the compressible material beyond its limits.

Suddenly Arvada realized the the whole pathetic futility of her desire.

She wanted to talk to Sahan one more time.

She wanted to put things back as they had been those last few sweet, sweet months. Sahan's death had collapsed her universe inside and out, leaving her with nothing but vengeance.

Thin gruel indeed, for the heart.

But even if Sahan lived, it would hardly be the Sahan she'd known. Certainly he would not have Sahan's body. No body at all, really, except the one the Evolved manufactured for him.

Even if she could somehow reach him through the holobrain, what would she find?

A weapon. A semi-human hunter-killer, programmed to hone in on one target.

Arvada Sattar.

This was foolish. She didn't even want a holobrain anymore. She'd be better off without it.

Only she couldn't let go.

Next to her Ligea Romero glanced at her curiously. Too conflicted to speak, Arvada raised a hand to indicate everything was all right.

Yeah. Frickin' brilliant.

"Captain," called Tarika, sitting at the central sensor console, flanked by two subordinates. "We still don't have visual, but I'm getting identifiable readings. Enemy ships. Five, six ... seven ... eight.... ten. Warships, clearly. Three or possibly four look like heavies. Plus some subsidiary disturbances I'm not sure of."

"Freighters," said Arvada. "To transport the Grinders. Catalan's crews don't want them aboard."

Ligea Romero grinned. "Close allies."

"Keep an eye on it, Tarika," Arvada said needlessly. She must be more nervous than she felt. "I want to know just how many heavies are with them."

"Aye, Captain."

If Tarika's initial estimate was correct — of course it was — the two sides would be evenly matched in line of battle ships, but Arvada would outnumber the Collaborationist cruisers handily.

The holobrain would be aboard one of the freighters. Along with the Grinders.

Arvada herself had requested six heavies, which would have ensured victory. But many of the heavy Captains were reluctant to leave the *Kepler* so lightly defended despite Arvada's assurances. So frustrating, the way so many insisted on fighting the war they'd been trained for rather than the war they were in.

Or maybe they simply did not want to accept her leadership, even if it meant sitting out the war while they sulked on their pristine bridges. Their vanity being more important than the fate of the Peregrine Alliance.

A flashing light on the swing console before her revealed that Solange O'Grady wanted to talk. Though Arvada was ostensibly fleet commander, Solange had retained overall command of the heavies. Another half-measure Arvada would just have to live with. Hell, as a Lieutenant Commander she shouldn't complain.

She slipped on her headset. "Captain O'Grady?"

"I presume you have the same readings we do."

"We do."

"I fully acknowledge you are in command. But how long do you want to wait before we reveal ourselves? For the heavies at least it wouldn't hurt to have the chance to jack up more momentum with a partial slingshot."

"Acknowledged. On the other hand, the closer they come the less room they'll have to maneuver around us. Presuming they choose not to fight, which is my assumption."

In truth she wanted to force the enemy into a balls-to-the-wall scramble. Where the survival imperative might place any orders not to let the holobrain fall into enemy hands low on their list of priorities.

"Very well," said Solange. "It's your party. When we do engage, I presume I still take my heavies straight against theirs and leave the cruisers to you."

My heavies.

"Just so. Thank you, Solange." The first name to remind her just who was in command.

"Sure thing. O'Grady out."

A bit curt, that. But no hint that Solange wouldn't do as told.

Didn't you just say that capturing a holobrain was foolishness?

So I did. But I want it.

Would you be so afraid the Evolved could turn Sahan against you if you'd treated him better the first time around?

Dammit, I did what I had to do! Sahan understood that.

Didn't lessen his pain much though, did it?

Shut up! I'm trying to think!

"Captain?"

Ligea, looking concerned. Arvada sniffed, then gave a curt nod. The second time she'd had to assure the XO her Captain was up to the job.

Ligea continued to stare at her.

"Yes, Number One?"

"I've been fighting this war ever since Sahan grabbed the *Mettalise.* There's still a lot I don't understand. But I've seen enough to know this. You *are* the war. If it was up to me, you'd be in charge of the whole goddamn fleet, and this goddamn war would be a lot closer to being won."

Lacking the words to reply, Arvada reached over and squeezed her hand.

***

To avoid detection Arvada ordered her force deeper toward the sun as Catalan's warships drew closer. Heat and radiation mounted. Though well above the solarsphere's critical zone, the prolonged build-up turned the interiors of the Alliance ships sweat-warm, introducing a bitter, close smell to the air. The hulls moaned and groaned and occasionally *cracked!* as pressure and differential expansion tugged at them. The engines had not yet started to hiccup, but aboard several of the cruisers they made snorting sounds from time to time.

Closer and closer the enemy drew, the data transmitted by stealth drones themselves skittering the depth where they could still get readings.

Four cigar-shaped, silver-plated line of battle ships formed a wide box within which the six sleek needle-nosed fast cruisers, with their stubby weapons wings extending from either side, darted like sheep dogs at the heels of the lumbering freighters. Those were Class C ships, their donut hulls slowly turning in lieu of inertial dampers to impart just enough centrifugal force to hold their cargo in place.

One of them would carry the holobrain. Not knowing which, Arvada's cruisers would have to board both. If they weren't blown up by their own forces.

When the enemy detected the Alliance fleet, and it couldn't be much longer, they would most likely attempt a looping course in a race to reach a Jump point with Rione before Arvada's ships could cut them off. Once in the solarsphere the battle would become confused and unpredictable; ships firing at fleet glimpses of each other, while normally sustainable hits could send a vessel tumbling down the gravitational well.

On the other hand, if the Alliance fleet attacked too soon, as Solange proposed, the Collaborationists might simply turn and run. Given a sufficient lead the Alliance fleet could not overhaul them. So long as the pursuit continued it would take both forces out of the war.

Solange O'Grady did not consider that a possibility. She could not accept that her fellow Captains, even on the other side, people whom she'd known since the Academy, might display such cowardice.

But to Arvada such a course would make perfect sense. Such a stalemate would extend the time the Evolved had to bring a new Master Holobrain, along with such warships and Grinders as they had in reserve, into the war.

Given such a possibility her own preference would have been to take the fleet further down, to a depth that would thoroughly muddle the enemy's sensors. But most of her Captains did not share her enthusiasm for skating around the sides of the gravitational well.

So she waited. Resisting the temptation to charge out as the heavies loomed so large on max magnification you could count the irising flanges around their weapons ports.

She waited until suddenly the enemy formation darted spinward, to her left.

"All personnel, helmets on," she ordered over the shipwide channel. Along the console platform pairs teamed up to help each other plug the shielded wiring of their helmet sensors into their ponytails. Ligea Romero came and stood by with Arvada's helmet in her hands.

Over the fleet channel she broadcast:

"ATTACK! Heavies attack heavies, cruisers attack cruisers. Wring everything you can out of your engines. It's more important to engage than to maintain formation."

Her ships clawed up out of Rione's gravity well, their redlining engines setting off trip-hammer shudders in the hulls. With *Geirovar* in the lead, they curved spinward, keeping themselves between the enemy and the sun. The Collaborationist fleet maintained a shrinking orbit in toward Rione, the Alliance a slightly expanding one. Catalan's ships had a greater distance to travel, but with gravity working in their favor they might still pull ahead just far enough to reach Jump.

Solange O'Grady called in. Since they were both wearing helmets, she and Arvada could transmit on a private channel that centered each other's voice in their brains.

"They certainly don't have much appetite for combat," O'Grady observed.

"I'm thinking Raisa Catalan may be running out of ships. Ones whose crews she trusts, anyway."

Solange barked a laugh that bounced painfully off the insides of Arvada's skull. "If not, she will be soon."

She was right. For a few minutes it looked as if the drag of pulling free of Rione's gravity might slow the Alliance fleet just enough to afford the Collaborationists a critical lead. Now, however, possessing the inner track was starting to tell. The chase had a way to go, and might yet prove a close-run thing, but collision appeared inevitable.

By now the two freighters lagged far behind.

Would the enemy just leave them there? Grinders were expendable, but allowing a holobrain to fall into Arvada's hands had caused the Evolved no end of trouble before.

"*Usagi, Bhimadevi*, take my wing." Leaving the channel open, she switched to Helm. "Home in on those freighters." Then to Olawenji Ferguson aboard the cruiser *Gotzone*: "You lead the attack against any enemy cruisers that don't try and pile up on my force."

"Acknowledged."

She didn't bother calling Captain O'Grady. Solange would do what she wanted to anyway.

As Arvada's three cruisers curved upward, two of the enemy cruisers began dropping back with the evident intention of destroying the freighters rather than letting them fall into her hands. Only a holobrain would make them risk themselves thus.

Arvada recognized the pair. The *Natessa* was under the command of Tane Wiritana, who'd graduated from the Academy a couple of years ahead of her. He'd seemed decent enough, if a bit too full of himself. But in their meetings since she found he'd acquired that stiff-necked air of self-importance that unfortunately came all too often with command.

The other enemy cruiser, the *Honiahaka*, was flown by Orzora Dowd, an older Captain who Arvada knew little of. But they hadn't given her the *Honiahaka*, one of the latest-generation cruisers, because she didn't know how to handle a ship.

Strange, thought Arvada, as she sat tense in her chair wondering which force would reach the freighters first, what a small world we all come from. Everyone had their own little cliques, but at root Academy graduates of any rank always seemed a family, with a family's unique understanding of each other that no outsider could ever achieve.

Now here they all were, dutifully trying to kill each other. Seemed like there should be a better way. Probably always did, to those hovering above the meatgrinder.

The two trailing enemy cruisers reversed thrust to allow the freighters to reach them more quickly

She opened a channel to her own detachment. "Prepare chaff. Rolling cloud, successive bursts. We'll lay down a field around the freighters the second we come into range. *Usagi*, spread yours ten kilometers ahead. *Bhimadevi*, five kilometers. Lieutenant Wainwright," she said to her Weapons Officer, "envelope both freighters."

Hopefully the chaff would disrupt the guidance systems on the incoming missiles. Though chancy, it wouldn't take much. This wasn't the solarsphere, where a proximity blast could transmit pressure waves of super-heated particles. Here an explosion must make direct contact to inflict damage. At space-battle velocities, even a fleeting misdirection might cause a missile to overshoot far enough to make recovery impossible.

Maybe.

Both cruisers fired a pair of shots rearward, the computer-enhanced streaks plainly visible on the bridge screen of the *Geirovar*. Arvada's cruisers fired off their chaff, running neck-in-neck toward the freighters. Both Arvada and the crews of the two freighters had an uncomfortably long time to watch their fate approach.

One of the freighters got lucky. Though the missile tracks appeared dead on a collision course from Arvada's angle, they somehow forked and streaked by, no doubt leaving the crews' hearts pounding even harder than her own. The freighter's commander, seeing enemy ships rising from below and equally deadly allies firing on him from straight ahead, turned from Rione, veering away on the sharpest angle he could, which to Arvada's eyes looked pathetically like a straight line.

The other freighter took a hit in the donut ring rotating about the central propulsion system. Arvada cursed aloud.

First a section of the circular hull disintegrated. Unbalanced, the freighter began to wobble.

"All ships, engage," Arvada ordered. The range had decreased to where the two enemy cruisers had to break off firing on the freighters to meet the Alliance attack.

Which was good news for the freighter performing its comic imitation of evasive maneuvers, but too late for the other. The great wheel went into a pendulum swing which appeared quite lazy from the *Geirovar* but generated stresses no hull could withstand. Section by section it disintegrated. Debris shot into space like a gray mist. The squat cylinder at the freighter's center, holding the engines and bridge, held intact for several minutes. Then the back-and-forth stresses transmitted through the spokes finally tore it open.

And the holobrain? If it had been in the doomed freighter, could it still survive?

She'd have to find out later. As the two enemy cruisers closed in, the remaining four cruisers from the Collaborationist fleet turned back to join in, the six of the *Gotzone* formation closing around them. All on a collision course.

No need for tactics. With sixteen cruisers darting about, firing and evading, any sentence she began would be irrelevant before she reached the end of it.

Time for the inspirational speech.

"Hunker down, people," she broadcast. "Time to do some shooting."

A few seconds later, the yellow streaks of missile trails formed a cage about the combatants.

Chapter 28

THE GRINDERS SPENT MOST of their lives in the training halls.

There were four halls that Sahan knew of. Two were vast caverns given over to zero-g practice. The interiors could be adjusted to various configurations. Sometimes they were left open for group-versus-group contests. At other times densely packed obstacles tested the Grinders' agility in suits and jetpacs. Which as Sahan had noted in his previous encounters with them, was never spectacular, but generally competent.

Two other halls featured Earth-normal gravity, which could be increased to nearly double for endurance training or down to one-quarter to mimic the conditions on many mining colonies or lesser habitats. Here the practice emphasized close combat with vibra-swords and of course the fearsome external teeth.

For the most part the Grinders trained in suits. No mystery there; it took Peregrines months of training to effectively utilize, let alone master, the logarithmically-scaled power suits without catapulting their training partner or themselves into solid objects.

And that was just to perform basic mechanical tasks. To wield the suit in the improvisational chaos of combat took more practice still. Less than half of Peregrines who began training as Marines completed it. The degree of sustained concentration necessary to utilize the suits' power effectively over such a wide and ever-changing range of situations was just too exhausting.

If Peregrines found the training too much, they at least had other lives open to them. The Grinders did not. Nor did they have effective hands-on training. They practiced against simulated enemies in feedback gear, and as they gained proficiency they practiced more and more against each other. But they totally lacked any practice in meditation or tai chi to sensitize them to their own bodies. The Peregrines mandated such training to all Riggers and Marines.

What the Grinders did have, courtesy of the Evolved, was aversive conditioning. If they failed to correctly make the adjustments indicated by their feedback systems, an electric shock sharpened their concentration. A crude tool, but given enough time, serviceable.

The Evolved had plenty of time. And the Grinders had plenty of pain.

Sahan's role became to act as what he thought of as a training dummy. Hour after hour the more advanced Grinders threw themselves at him. Only to be clubbed down with the hard plastic weapons they trained with or hurled straight-out-horizontal five meters or more across the floor.

He didn't wear a suit for these exercises.

The Grinders were, of course, terrified of him.

Small wonder. Apart from the beatings he inflicted upon them, all four high walls of the training hall showed vids of Sahan Kotori in his earlier incarnation as a Peregrine opening their insides or otherwise causing their heads to explode.

Though his face now mirrored theirs, the Grinders knew full well who he was.

Of course the body-camera scenes were not all of him, though the Grinders believed them to be. He'd have to spend close to a year in unbroken combat to generate so much blood-splattered melodrama.

But among the Grinders independent thought was not encouraged. They believed all that mayhem they saw on the walls of the training halls came courtesy of Sahan Kotori. And his brutal domination of them in his new uber-Grinder form confirmed it.

For all their fear, the Grinders never made any move to sweep over him in a rush. Such an irresistible anger would only be instilled by the holobrain. And while it might drive them to the edge of fury, only in specific instances would it drive them beyond. The Evolved just didn't have so many Grinders they could afford to waste them against Sahan.

So the holobrains kept the hormonal flow and stimulation to various brain centers at a level somewhere between aggression and suicide.

At times he could see himself reflected through their eyes. Another effect of the holobrain. And because of their conditioning, he occasionally saw himself not in the Grinder form he wore, but as Sahan Kotori, the erstwhile human they were trained to fear.

And he wanted to rip that man's guts out. With his new Grinder teeth.

Because beneath the sound of battle-screeches and howls of pain, he heard Arvada's mocking laughter.

That laughter caused many a Grinder injuries of a degree Sahan knew were excessive to the circumstances.

He was so terribly sick of it. Arvada's laughter, his own hatred, the rage deflected onto hapless opponents.

He had trouble thinking of anything beyond killing her. For revenge, to stop the pain, but most of all just to quiet the harpy cry of her laughter he could not scrape from his ears.

Chapter 29

THE *GEIROVAR* DRIFTED IN space.

On the bridge, about half the lights and monitors functioned on the emergency power supply. The rest had been shaken into dysfunction, mountings torn out of the walls and ceiling, wires ripped from their moorings.

The wet stale-laundry smell of fire suppressant mixed with the ozone-rich, nostril-scratching stench of burnt wires and plastics. Pools of every liquid piped anywhere on the ship added their own stomach-wrenching stink as they were blown through the ship by a life support system gone dingo.

Arvada's suit filtered out some but not all of the smells. As soon as she had the situation halfway under control and knew what was going on where, she should start rotating personnel. Presuming, that is, there were still enough less-toxic areas of the *Geirovar* left to give anyone a breather.

At intervals new fires would hiss and spark among the bridge consoles, and need to be smothered by white-suited figures jetting to and hovering over the site because the inertial dampers were out. Clouds of white mist from the suppressants floated ghost-like about the bridge, hosting black twists of acrid smoke from the electrical fires.

Damage control reports flooded her earphones, since so many sections of the ship could not longer be visually transmitted onto the screens. Arvada tried to sort out the priorities, all expressed to her in identical states of near panic. To hear it from the people on the scene, the whole ship was burning, disintegrating, evacuating atmosphere, or simply inert.

"Malaika, I have to know *now*," she told the Chief Engineer. "Will we have propulsion, and when?"

"I understand the urgency, Captain," came the voice, predominating over the others within her head, "but I have nothing like functioning diagnostics here."

"Then guess." The Engineer's least favorite word.

"Very well. My guess is, no. Before we even know for sure what's wrong we'll have to tear into the engines manually. And my *guess* is we won't like what we see. I could be wrong. Maybe the pounding jarred loose a couple/three integral systems, and we can have propulsion back in a few hours. But I'll be surprised."

"I see. Thank you. Do what you can."

She switched over to Ligea Romero, and rather to her surprise, got visual on her chair monitor. Of a sort. Suited figures flew in and out of a smoke cloud that hid them within a couple of meters. Though she saw no flame, Arvada cringed anyway. Her impulse was to get those people out of there. But it was Ligea on the scene, in charge of the damage control party.

"Ligea, this is the Captain. Tell me."

A suited figure in the corner of the picture, holding by her toes to a twisted sheet of metal, looked up from where she'd been in intense conversation with two others.

"Oh wow," she said. "Visual's back. Great. Kind of. Well, Captain, it's what you see. We look to have the main fire under control, but spot fires keep erupting. I'd say we're on top of it for now, so long as no one kicks the walls too hard. If you're asking when you might have Weapons back, my best estimate is, never. It's difficult to get a complete picture through all the smoke, but no one's come back so far to say they found an undamaged section."

"Thank you, Ligea." No Weapons, no propulsion, no inertial dampers. Vacuum claiming at least a third of the ship, and where atmosphere held, it was poisonous. Not to mention fires still breaking out from bow to stern for obscure reasons of their own.

On the one functioning main screen all Arvada could see of the battle was the three twisted lumps of the *Honiahaka* drifting nearby, home to nothing but vacuum and corpses. Seeing the Collaborationist cruisers outnumbered, Orzora Dowd had come straight as a jousting knight for the *Geirovar*. Clearly by killing Arvada she hoped to demoralize the enemy.

Bravely done. Panache galore. But Arvada still lived.

As for the *Geirovar*....

She went shipwide.

"Everyone, this is the Captain. You have fought bravely. But it is my judgment that the *Geirovar* is too badly damaged either to attain Jump or to survive it. I am therefore giving the order to abandon ship. I repeat, abandon ship. Those who can't make it to the hangar bay, take to the escape pods. You know the drill. Section heads, make sure everyone on your team gets the word. Security, you will help evacuate the wounded from all over the ship. Damage control, gather under the direct supervision of the First Officer. Commander Romero, your first task is to determine no one gets trapped anywhere. Keep in contact with me at all times."

I don't want to leave my ship!

You are doing what must be done. You are doing what must be done. You are doing what must be done.

First the *Viveca*, now—

You are doing what must be done.

"I repeat. Abandon ship."

Chapter 30

Days and nights did not exist for him. Sahan would get an impulse to go here, or go there, to eat, to fight, to sleep. These impulses had nothing to do with any conscious will.

He didn't care. While he was impatient to get to Arvada, to rip the laughter from her mouth and out of his head, he had long experience of military life. Things happened when they happened. You waited forever, trained forever. Then when the action finally began, found yourself never quite prepared.

Eventually he followed an impulse that told him to go to one of the training halls and climb a set of outside stairs. He entered onto a small railed platform at mid-level.

The space was dark except for sparkling pools of light floating above and below. The irregular light revealed a dim pattern that slowly resolved into open-sided pyramids stacked head to toe; the shock-absorbing buttresses common to all space construction. The pyramids reached four meters high. Each leg of the triangular base ran about three meters.

He smelled blood, though there was no sign blood had yet been shed.

Disconnected fragments of memory rushed at him. Sahan waved his artificial hands to fend them off. He had no good memories.

They possessed him anyway. The Sector Seal aboard the … something. Where he'd led a force of Marines and Riggers into massacre.

An initial impression of silence quickly revealed an underlying shuffling sound.

Grinders. Pressing in amid the dark pools between flares.

His mind reeled with a mix of memories and the situation developing around him. He could not separate the two. He heard the slicing howl of battle-saws and vibra-swords ripping through armor, the high-pitched whine of flechettes ricocheting off beams. Heard desperate voices calling to him for help when he had no help to give.

He heard the cries turn to screams.

First from the living.

Then from the dead.

WHY?

The accusations came as a barrage from decapitated heads.

WHYWHYWHY….

Arvada's laughter rippled through his brain. He saw suited Grinders crawling toward him along the beams. Now, or then? They snarled and crouched and came stalking from pyramid to pyramid. In the scattered, sparkling light of flares their white suits and creeping progress resembled albino spiders.

Confusion. He had no suit. But aboard the *Enodia*….

Wherever he was, this artificial Grinder body (it must be the present, the present, but he was having such a hard time hanging onto it) was nearly as strong.

WHYWHYWHY….

Sahan jumped to the top of the railing. He laughed, as well as this mix of organics and metals could; a percussive, ratcheting sound. Combat, real combat with real death, was the only balm for his pain.

He leapt into the nearest pyramid. Three Grinders already held it. Two stood on the base beams and a third clung to one of the slanting uprights. He saw no weapons besides their teeth, but in suits those were formidable enough.

The three froze in place, cowed by his sudden appearance despite the stimulants coursing through their brains.

From all around came Grinder battle-screeches. Inside his brain it morphed into Arvada's laughter.

DIE! she cried. Die and be done with it. These creatures will *eat* you. And I shall laugh to watch.

Will you? Watch then, and laugh if you can.

With his left arm he grabbed the Grinder clinging to the upright and plucked him loose. Suited up, the Grinder was very strong; it reached clawing fingers toward his face but Sahan was taller and longer-limbed and fully as strong. He smashed the Grinder back against the beam, then hurled its limp body into the one to his right. The Grinder screamed as he was knocked off his perch into a long bouncing fall. The third fled to an adjoining pyramid.

Two more jumped in from either side. Sahan swung around the beam to his left and as the newly-planted Grinder tried to turn to meet him, stiff-armed him into another caroming fall. He jumped to the adjacent pyramid where he grabbed another Grinder at chest and crotch, hoisted him overhead, and hurled him at two more rushing him. The three went tumbling down together.

That still didn't stop Arvada's laughter. Or the relentless cries of WHY?

The next few moments were a blur of sound and motion and jarring impact and emotion so strong his sight flickered into black and white. But his body reacted to its own reflexes.

At last the Grinders fell back. Sahan didn't know how many he'd killed, but he could feel their mood. Their hate no longer equaled their fear.

He realized he was not aboard the *Enodia*, but the Evolved ship. He'd known it all along. Hadn't he? Just not quite settled into it.

Why had the Grinders attacked him? Had the Evolved wanted him dead they had more direct and less costly ways.

But the Evolved weren't satisfied by bouts in the training hall. They wanted Sahan to master the Grinders. And for that a sacrifice had to be made.

Now the Grinders cringed and sulked, and avoided his eyes.

Triumph coursed through his mind, riding on thoughts of vengeance.

But it did not take complete hold. Because almost at once an even stronger wave of revulsion swept over him.

Puppets. They were all puppets. Him and the Grinders alike. He'd always been a puppet. First Arvada's, now the Evolved's.

Her laughter returned.

Watch the puppets slay each other. So funny, that mix of passion and futility. Comic perversions of humanity, with not a one of them, not Sahan, not the Grinders, possessing a single scrap of a soul worth a moment's pity. Nothing but amusement. Bug-eyed monsters, suited to be mowed down as if in a video game.

He swung through the pyramids toward the platform. The Grinders scrambled out of his way.

He could not make a speech, even had he known what to say. The Grinders did possess language, but of limited scope. Like Sahan, their life was regulated through images and impulses instilled by the holobrains. From what he could glean of their perceptions through overlap from the holobrains, their existence tended toward the dreamlike; a constant reaction to shifting inputs. All the major ones generated by the holobrains.

If any baseline emotion characterized the Grinders, Sahan perceived it as shame. They were the rejected ones. The ones cast out of heaven. The ones who must pay for past sins they did not even understand. All this had he seen during the funeral-turned orgy.

But underneath it all lay a longing not initiated or controlled by the holobrains.

Now the Grinders faced him silent and subdued, as if waiting for judgment.

The pain (PAIN!) began to trickle through him. More a warning than the real thing; enough to fold up an ordinary human perhaps, but of no great moment to Sahan.

He probed harder.

The pain intensified. A barrage of electroshocks at vulnerable points of his body that had no real existence outside his brain, but felt most real. Elbows, knees, fingers; groin, liver, heart. Sahan heard his Grinder teeth rattle as his body spasmed.

This was more serious. More distracting. Still he stood, gripping the railing for support.

The Grinders pressed tighter together before the platform. Some standing, some clinging to the uprights. By now their longing was palpable. Where had he seen/felt something like it before?

Now fire reinforced the electroshock, spreading along what would have been his bones did he have any. The steel rail fronting the platform whined softly from the pressure of his quivering hands.

WE ARE THE SAME. WE ARE THE HATED ONES. YOU, AND I.

That's what he tried to tell them with all the force of will he marshalled to fight through the pain.

Sahan himself did not know exactly what he meant. He was talking to the Grinders, he was talking to the severed heads screaming WHY? He was talking to his own fragmented saga, split across different bodies, different realities in life and the holobrains.

WE ARE ONE.

The pain flared worse. Losing control of his limbs, Sahan slowly sank to his knees.

The Grinders watched him passively. But in their minds, activity took place that was for once outside the province of the holobrains. The Evolved tried to divert it, but a fascination, a hunger spread through them.

Sahan did not understand it; the Grinders did not understand it. But it pulled them toward some common point invisibly far off.

He was jerking now, exhalations hammering out of him because he lacked the strength to scream. He could no longer see around the PAIN.

But he heard a refrain snaking through his agony; no more than a thin little wail to him but a torrential outburst among

the Grinders. They might not wholly understand it, but some meaning lurking within the words still compelled them:
    WE ARE ONE.

Chapter 31

Handing her helmet off to one of the *Dysis* crew, Arvada Sattar dismissed the escort of two Marines and found her own way from the hangar bay onto the bridge. She still wore her suit. She'd needed it, getting off the *Geirovar*. Black fire streaks formed tiger stripes over the blue fabric.

"Welcome aboard, Captain Sattar," said Solange O'Grady, rising with a broad, freckled, and just slightly patronizing smile from the Captain's chair. "Congratulations on your victory."

"Thank you, Captain O'Grady."

Arvada noted Solange did not say "the bridge is yours." Arvada might be in over-call command of the raid on the Rione system, but Solange regarded the line of battle ships as sacred ground. *Her* sacred ground. In her eyes Arvada Sattar commanded no more than a detachment of fast cruisers. Solange O'Grady was, after all, a senior Captain going on Admiral, to Arvada's official rank of Lieutenant Commander.

Arvada gave her a nod of acknowledgment. The fleet council that gave her leadership for this battle had left unsettled the prickly matter of who should first salute who.

Arvada checked the screen curving around the front of the bridge. There hung the *Geirovar*, dead and drifting. Her ship. From this perspective the cruiser didn't look so bad. A few rents in the hull, one of the weapons wings gone, one of the engines an open view into a salvage yard. Almost peaceful, really.

And yet how sweet the air here aboard *Dysis*, free of the stench of burning wires and plastics! How clear the view, without half the lights out, the rest flickering on a battered backup system, and acrid clouds of smoke drifting across everything. How peaceful, without the ear-piercing electric hiss and the ship falling apart while five dozen people shouted in your earphones demanding to know what to do about it. How nice to plant your feet firmly on the deck, with the inertial dampers still functioning so you didn't have to keep dodging the floating debris blown loose and bouncing off the walls.

And how it hurt, to watch a ship that had given its all for her, lying crippled and helpless, waiting to be put from its pain.

"Captain O'Grady, have the *Geirovar* destroyed, if you please."

Without a word Solange climbed the steps to the platform running around the bridge. She whispered some words into the ear of her Weapons officer, softly so that Arvada would not have to hear.

Arvada kept her eyes focused on the screen while tension kept her at close to full attention. The end was anti-climactic. Solange must have ordered visual tracking turned off on the missiles. Suddenly there was an explosion where the *Geirovar* had been. Then a shimmering cloud of dust, then nothing but a distant background of stars, settling back into stillness following the quickly dissipating wave of heat.

"Thank you," said Arvada, straining to keep her voice level. Some might criticize her for the decision to destroy the

Geirovar. They'd see pictures, and insist the ship could have been saved.

But even if they somehow patched up the one relatively intact engine, dubious in itself, the cruiser would never survive the gravitational stresses involved in Jump.

Arvada knew she was right. She just had to keep telling herself, the way you'd keep telling yourself a faithful but old and crippled dog's time had finally come.

Solange came back. She wore fatigues, as did her crew. They would have been suited up for the battle. But Solange had declared the battle won.

"My crew?" Arvada asked the Captain of the *Dysis*, twelve years her senior. "There was too much radio interference in the sled to keep close track."

"Everyone who exited the *Geirovar* in sleds or pods survived," Solange told her. "Most are here. The others have been picked up or will be within minutes by the *Bhimadevi* or *Usagi*."

"Good. Very good. Thank you."

"The wounded are being cared for, and so far no new fatalities have been reported. As for those killed aboard the *Geirovar*....?" She raised her eyebrows, giving Arvada a chance to stop her.

"I know." Twenty-nine. Twenty-nine crew whose faces and voices and teamwork she knew so well.

It could have been worse. Was worse, for Orzora Dowd, who lost her entire crew, along with her ship and her life, when she hurled the *Honiahaka* straight at the *Geirovar*. Arvada did not believe Orzora had been even halfway trying to survive that mad attack. She just meant to take Arvada out with her; to deprive the Alliance of their most famous battle commander.

Surprising that such loyalty still remained among the followers of the traitor Raisa Catalan. Or maybe she had simply been unable to surrender her ship without one last all-out effort. As Arvada would have been.

"If you would bring me up to date, Captain?" she asked Solange. In private they were on a first-name basis. But with the question of command so ambiguous between them, in such a formal setting they remained relatively formal.

"A complete victory," Solange said with an ear-to-ear grin. She was normally a severe, bony woman with bristly bright red hair, formidable jaw, and severe, sunken cheeks, a woman who if she had a sense of humor preferred to keep it to herself. But now she positively lit up.

"Our cruisers were of course successful," she said, the "of course" there to remind Arvada the enemy cruiser force had after all been outnumbered almost two to one. "You destroyed the *Honiahaka* in the *Geirovar*. *Usagi* and *Lyngheid* crippled and took the *Melusina*. The *Natessa* surrendered. Pretty much without firing a shot."

That was a surprise. "Tane Wiritana's ship?"

"Exactly. I always said the smug bastard was a big bag of wind. The final cruiser somehow eluded our ships and made it to Jump. But we chalked up four out of five, one of them intact."

"And the — your — heavies?" Why not? She was standing on Captain O'Grady's bridge.

"Much the same. One enemy got away from us, with considerable damage. Of the other three, we took them all. Including" — she spread her hands in a most un-O'Gradyish flourish — "the *Druga*."

"Raisa Catalan's flagship?" Arvada had a moment of light-headedness as a mix of hate and hope erupted upward. "*Please* tell me she was on board. Oh, I'd *so* love to take that woman into the Decahedron. Just for a friendly bout, understand. No mistreatment of prisoners."

Solange chuffed, probably meant to be a laugh. Arvada Sattar's "friendly" bouts had been something of a legend, not so long ago.

"You'll have to wait for that, I'm afraid. Catalan never left Harrar's Reach. Can't say the *Druga* did her proud. Neither did the *Megara*. They fired off a few shots, took a little damage — nothing a fresh coat of paint won't fix — then surrendered. You were right about the state of morale in the Collaborationist fleet. Unfortunately the third heavy, *Callia*, didn't come out of it so well. Cooked up with all hands. Unlike the rest of them, Captain Beaufort was a fighter. A good man, before he chose the wrong side."

"I'm sorry," said Arvada, sensing a personal connection.

"I'm not. I do respect him and his crew, though. These other Captains who haul down the flag when you toss a firecracker at them, what can you say? First traitors, then cowards, now begging for the chance to be traitors again. For years I said the Navy had its head stuck up its ass, making Captains out of clerks. No wonder we had to put a born pirate in command."

Arvada ignored that. "And our own ships?"

"The *Rajni* took a bit of a beating. Mainly the *Callia's* doing. I think she can be refitted, if we can hold on to the repair facilities at the *Kepler*. But I wouldn't count on her any time soon. The rest of us, all we need is a few bolts tightened and a few new parts here and there. Like I said, it was hardly the Battle of Trafalgar."

In truth Solange had performed brilliantly. All very well to say the enemy heavies didn't fight that hard; they very well might have had Solange not swept down on them like a runaway asteroid. She was a true fighting Captain, whom most might have expected to gain the reputation Arvada Sattar held now, as the great hero of the Resistance.

But two factors had held Solange back. The first was that like most of the senior officers, she'd followed tradition and stayed too obedient too long to both Naval Command and the Citizens' Council, even after it became clear both bodies were more concerned with avoiding war than fighting it.

The second, of course, was that unlike Arvada, Solange never had Sahan Kotori.

Which brought up the whole subject of this exercise, though none but Arvada yet knew.

"One of the freighters was destroyed by its own cruisers," she said. "What of the other?" She'd been too busy dodging missiles from the *Honiahaka* to track it.

"Hove to, surrounded by our cruisers. The Peregrine crew are begging to be taken off and made prisoner. They're probably scared of all the Grinders aboard. I would be. Wayland Takedi of the *Keyna* has ordered them to remain in place pending further orders from you."

"Good." Once the Peregrine crew was off, they might set some auto-destruct behind them. "I want to go there. We are going to take the freighter. I will lead the attack, using Marines from the *Dysis* and *Keyna*. You of course have command of the fleet should I be lost."

Solange frowned. "*You'll* lead the attack? Sorry, but I must have missed something here. What attack are we talking about? I assumed we would take the crew off the freighter, then dust it along with the Grinders inside. You're talking about boarding and fighting them?"

A little more overt respect would have been nice. Once again Arvada declined to get sidetracked in authority squabbles.

"There is something aboard that freighter I want. A holobrain, in fact."

"Ah, a holobrain."

Solange's narrow lips pursed in an effort to remain noncommittal. She was plainly underwhelmed by this pseudo-mystical holobrain claptrap no one but *maybe* Arvada understood. And to which no one would offer the slightest credence had not Sahan Kotori, Arvada's late XO — and lover, scandalously — worked some wizardry through them to destroy an Evolved heavy. Of course Sahan, the former Dainichi, was widely regarded as an unsavory mix of madman and mystic.

"I did have my Marines stand down just a few minutes ago," she told Arvada. "There didn't appear anyone left to fight."

"Order them to suit up again, if you please."

"Will they be boarding directly, or—"

"We shall see. Now if you would be so good, Captain O'Grady, I would ask you to lay us alongside the freighter."

"Yes, of course." Solange turned aside to issue the appropriate orders to move the *Dysis* to the freighter's position.

"But I might suggest," she told Arvada, "that if there is an Evolved holobrain aboard that freighter, that aside from being surrounded by Grinders, it might just possibly auto-destruct the moment you get near. You know more about these things than I do, of course. More than anyone." And thank God for that, the sideways shift of her green eyes suggested. "But I believe the possibility should be considered."

"That," said Arvada, "is why I'm leading the recovery party."

***

"Suit up," Arvada told Beck.

The Evolved looked up from the bench uncomprehending. "Suit up?"

"You people *do* use suits in EVA, don't you?"

"EVA? Why would I be going EVA? What are you talking about?" One of the Marines sitting at either side nudged his arm with her elbow, not gently. "Captain Sattar," he added, rubbing the sore spot.

Before the battle, this bay aboard the *Dysis* had been configured to accommodate any spill-over from the med section, as well as a resting place for survivors from lost ships. None of the beds and stations lining the far wall was in use; the *Dysis* had taken few casualties. Even with the most of the *Geirovar's* wounded aboard, sick bay could hold the wounded.

Now the survivors rested in rows of acceleration couches bolted to the floor plates, or helped each other off with their suits, hanging them on extensions at the back of the couches, ready to hand. Crew members of the *Dysis*, relieved from battle stations, circulated among them, handing out drinks and food, here and there checking vital signs, and absorbing thrilling accounts.

Solange O'Grady might stand down her crew, thinking the battle safely over, but Arvada still had work to do. So Solange would just have to suit up her Marines. But Arvada's own people had been through enough. Let them sip their coffee and gobble down pastry here among the soothing violet walls. Some of the scenes aboard the *Geirovar* would stay with them for years.

Burn marks on the suits gave off an acrid scent. An unpleasant reminder, to people who might have seen their comrades seared to death, or suffocated by toxic smoke too thick for their suits to filter out, or crushed by free-floating wreckage. But they kept the suits close nonetheless, because having just escaped one wreck, they were not ready to trust to anything.

A couple of Evolved heavies booming out of Jump could indeed justify all fears. But they wouldn't. The Evolved would not risk combat until another Master Holobrain was installed in Harrar's Reach. If the living Evolved should be killed before, their "souls" or whatever remained after the functional death of their bodies would be incorporated not in the Group Mind, but the Terror Barrier.

According to Beck, no new Master Holobrain had yet arrived.

Could she trust him? Did he know?

All Arvada trusted was his fear of the Terror Barrier. And his conviction that if he betrayed her, Arvada or one of her crew would kill him, the rules of war be hanged.

Why not? It was true.

Taking the holobrain in the freighter, surrounded as it was by Grinders, would be dangerous. But she needed it. She could not tell anyone why.

Beck had told her Sahan still lived. Some part of him, anyway.

Why would the Evolved go to the trouble of reviving an enemy on the very border of death? A man whose body had been so burned and battered as to be beyond all hope of salvage?

To use as a weapon against her.

And if Sahan did come against her, Arvada had no confidence she could stop him.

Unless, just maybe, she could somehow reach him first. And revive the love that once bound them.

Beck insisted it would make no difference. Even if she could communicate with Sahan through the holobrain, the Evolved now controlled his mind totally.

That's what Beck thought. No doubt the Evolved believed it too, and their power could not be denied.

Except maybe when it came to Sahan.

Arvada had to maintain that faith. Her love would not allow her to abandon him, no matter how dangerous to her he had become. To lose him to death, well, she'd already lived through that loss once. This was war.

But to the Terror Barrier, that she could not accept. *Would* not accept.

If she was to have any chance at all of reaching him, either in this world or beyond, she needed a holobrain.

Now here one waited for her.

Beck was making a fuss.

"You surely don't mean to take *me* out there, do you?" he said, waving a hand to indicate the vacuum beyond the *Dysis'* hull, where all sorts of dangers held sway. "Not aboard that freighter. How do you mean to deal with the Grinders?"

"Like I always do. Kill them."

"Oh, kill them." Beck rolled his eyes at this further demonstration of the barbarisms he'd come to expect from

Arvada Sattar. "And if in the midst of this blood-orgy the holobrain chooses to self-destruct?"

Arvada grabbed the front of his fatigues. To the pair of Marines she'd assigned to look after him she said: "Bring his suit."

She dragged him into the corridor, where she stood him up against the wall. Despite his slender build, Arvada knew the tall Evolved to be both strong and quick. But he was hardly likely to attack her here.

"You told me," she said, "that the holobrain would not self-destruct if it sensed you close enough to be killed."

"*Probably*, is in fact the word I used."

"Probably is good enough for me."

Beck tried to maintain a show of calm on his slender, ascetic face. "I further said that should a Master Holobrain have arrived in Peregrine space, the server brain would have no such compunction."

"Because the Master would bring you into the Group Mind instead of the Terror Barrier, right?"

"Broadly, yes. Probably."

"And has one arrived?"

He fixed his blue-gray eyes on hers, clearly wondering what the prospects were for attempting fairy tales. Arvada shook her head to warn him.

"I don't *think* so. I don't feel anything of the sort. But that might not be conclusive. Events are never so simple as you would like, Captain Sattar."

"Actually, they're simple as can be. We'll either live, or we'll die. Together."

"Captain, it is quite against the rules of war to force a prisoner into a combat zone."

"Force? A short time ago you were begging me to find you a holobrain. Spouting all sorts of wild accusations about torture and whatnot. So in order to avoid any perception that I might ever mistreat a prisoner, I have decided to grant your wish. We will now obtain for you a holobrain. Consider yourself fortunate to have such a humane captor. You did volunteer, did you not?"

She turned to the senior of the two Marines still holding the sections of Beck's suit. "You heard him volunteer, didn't you, Sergeant?"

"Loud and clear, Captain."

"There," she said. "All squared away. Sergeant Latumba and Corporal Trennan here will help you into your suit. You will then accompany us to the hangar bay, where we will board a landing craft along with personnel from the *Dysis* to secure the holobrain."

"Captain Sattar, will you *please* consider the consequences should I be killed? If you or your people die, they die. Should that be the only risk facing me, I should most willingly join you for the chance of obtaining the holobrain."

He was lying, but she let it go.

"But that," he said, "is hardly the case. You know that. If *I* die—"

"Yes, yes, I know. Gloom and doom. Hey, *I* didn't create the Terror Barrier. That's your lot. If you're going to create minefields for yourselves, you'll just have to find your own way through them. So now that we have that all settled, let's suit up and get going."

"Captain Sattar, you are spouting inanities. In the name of humanity I ask—"

"Unless of course you are too badly injured."

"Injured?"

"Yes, injured during the evacuation of the *Geirovar*. One of those internal injuries where at first no one notices anything, then suddenly poof! — you drop down dead on the spot. Ruptured spleen, ruptured kidney, who knows? Like right in this hall here." She glanced sidelong at the Marines. "You didn't hear that."

"Hear what, Sir?" Sergeant Latumba asked innocently, while Corporal Trennan studied the blank wall.

Beck sighed ostentatiously. "That a thinking, feeling being, more or less, could condemn me to the horrors of the Terror Barrier ... you really have no imagination at all, do you, Captain Sattar?"

"How much imagination do I need, when I have you?"

Chapter 32

THE BATTLE FOR THE holobrain degenerated into a real furball. Grinders and Marines zipped about the ragged section of hull that held the holobrain like opposing swarms of flies.

Arvada had allowed the freighter's crew to evacuate after bringing the rotation of the ring to a halt. They were quick to identify which section of the wheel contained the holobrain.

By then the Grinders, knowing no one was likely to take them prisoner, were pouring into space from all around the ring's circumference to defend the holobrain.

Arvada led the flight of sleds launched from the *Dysis* and the cruisers *Lyngheid*, *Usagi*, and *Keyna*. All the craft were stuffed beyond maximum listed capacity with Marines, with a contingent of now-veteran Riggers to make up the shortfall. This time she turned the piloting over to someone else while she sat in the aft chair, concentrating on the screens spread across her console.

Beck, suited up in an Alliance suit unfamiliar to him, was strapped in with the others back in the personnel bay, and most unhappy about it. He kept his recriminations to himself, however. Mainly because he was unable to interface with the suit sensors and Arvada had shut down all his comm channels but the ones direct to her and Sergeant Latumba, who with Corporal Trennan still shadowed him.

She directed the sleds to within five hundred meters of the freighter.

"Solange," she transmitted to the Captain of the *Dysis*, "break me off that segment containing the holobrain. Leave a little margin to either side, if you please. We don't want to bang it around any harder than we have to."

A moment later two missile trails streaked past the sled's cockpit, rather nearer than good manners might dictate. Just Solange affording her commander pro temp a little thrill. The yellow streaks headed to either side of the section containing the holobrain. The Grinders hovering around the area scattered frantically.

Two five-meter sections of pebble-surfaced brown hull disintegrated, leaving jagged ends. More suited Grinders poured from the cavities like bees from the hive. Debris from the explosion clattered off the nose of the sled, one larger piece causing Arvada to duck reflexively.

"Excellent, Captain O'Grady," she called. "Now take out the remaining sections of the wheel."

She waited for the salvo to wreak its havoc, leaving a cloud of debris, pieces of bodies, and a few short, spinning sections of hull behind. It should have killed a good number of Grinders, but many escaped because they'd already been swarming toward the holobrain.

"Sleds, close to within one hundred meters of the detached section. At one hundred meters we attack."

The sleds closed, halted at the specified distance. Their upper halves clamshelled open, disgorging over three hundred Marines. Quickly assuming formation, they jetted toward the Grinders circling the section of hull holding the holobrain.

***

ARVADA PERCEIVED THE BATTLE more through her sensors than her eyes. The center of her brain filled with a three-dimensional sphere dense with stabbing red heat trails from the exhaust of the jetpacs. The actual bodies of Grinders and Marines came through as faded blobs of rust propelled like arrowheads at the end of the crimson shafts. Their passage left short yellow mouse trails from her motion detectors. The only way to tell her people from the enemy was the silver-flashing transponders worn by the Marines.

Exiting the sleds the Marines formed up in a matrix, each suit at five meter intervals. Close enough for mutual support should the fighting turn hand-to-hand, yet spread out far enough that a near miss from a rocket didn't automatically track your comrade. It also allowed space for evasive action without knocking the nearest Marine's helmet off or getting tangled jetpac to jetpac.

The formation was also designed to keep unit fire pointed outward. Friendly fire was a major factor in space battles. Tracked rockets might swerve from the Marine's transponders in time, but once fired, flechettes were strictly a to-whom-it-may-concern proposition. And tricky to dodge because they came so fast and left neither heat nor guidance signature.

To Arvada's grave disappointment, the matrix broke down almost at once. Initially spread wide, the Grinders came hard for the Marine formation in corkscrewing loops. They took heavy casualties but the survivors got in. For the first few moments a near-Brownian motion broke out as fighters bounced off each other.

Then as Marines and Grinders alike sought room to maneuver, the fight broke down to dodge, chase, fire, and if you were lucky, evade any incoming missiles through your own effort before the suit took over, perhaps saving your life but not infrequently inflicting concussion as a side benefit.

Soon many of the Marines were twisting and turning with the foe in old-time dogfights. Though both sides were pretty evenly matched in speed and maneuverability, the aiming systems on the Marines' rockets and flechette rifles had a considerable edge tracking a fast-moving enemy. The evasive response of the Marines' suits was also superior. And with much of the freighter being destroyed, taking the Grinders there with it, they had a substantial advantage in numbers.

All around her Marines and Grinders chased each other, trying to swing inside the enemy's turning radius while firing from near contortionist poses. Several times Arvada saw grisly parades where the fleeing quarry would suddenly vibrate to the burst of a rocket or the piercing of flechettes, while half a second later their killer would suffer the same fate. Often the victor would immediately become the victim of another enemy cutting in behind while their attention was still fixed on the quarry.

"Don't get fixated on one target!" she shouted, mentally. "Keep your head on a swivel and stay paired up!" The sensors gave a clear 360-degree view, but task saturation was a not uncommon result.

"And cut the frickin' chatter!" She doubted anyone heard her. Her audio centers were filled with screams, shouts for help, shouts of triumph, shouts of terminal surprise.

A Grinder flew at her firing a rocket launcher. Arvada twisted away from the trail of fire, a half physical, half mental action. The projectile exhaust swerved toward her, but she'd switched ends during the evasion and was swooping back toward her attacker faster than the projectile could turn.

Swiftly closing, they both spun around in barrel rolls to throw off the other's projectiles. Playing chicken with a Grinder was not generally a high-percentage move; if they ever had any fear reflex it disappeared in battle.

Yet her aiming system sent a bundle of darts into his chest before his rockets could track her circular attack. A ball of mist puffed from his suit amid fibrillating tatters. As she shot past she saw his head pulped inside his helmet.

More missiles speared toward her; a squeezing field of scarlet lines appearing impossible to dodge. She rolled away from an indeterminate number, then her suit took over. She shook like a motor with its bearings gone.

Arvada came out of it dazed, unable to impose a pattern on all the bodies twisting around and the red missile tracks and silver streaks of flechette bundles going by. For some reason the left side of her jaw hurt like she'd taken a hard punch.

A pinch in her upper leg told her the suit was injecting stimulants. Her head cleared, became eager. But it still took her a near-fatal moment to try to derive some pattern amid the action surrounding her.

Don't fixate don't fixate don't—

She watched two deadly trains of Grinder-Marine-Grinder-Marine whizz by.

Above, in a somewhat more open patch she saw a Grinder jetting slowly, rocket launcher advanced on its shoulder swivel, searching for a target.

Arvada zoomed in the opposite direction. Swinging clear of several group fights and any number of missiles, she looped wide and came in behind the Grinder she'd spotted. When she caught sight of him he was speeding up, zoning in on a swooping, spherical fight involving half a dozen suits from both sides.

She extended her flechette rifle. At twenty yards targeting got a lock. She fired. Half a second later the Grinder went into that paroxysm that marked the death-flutter of an irredeemably punctured suit.

But by then she was in a wild curve away, in case someone was tracking her in turn. Resisting the temptation to use her eyes, Arvada tried to make sense of the crisscrossing lines of red and green depicted inside her skull. With an effort of will she slammed down against the sense of vulnerability common to large-scale space battles, where flechettes spreading out from their initial bundle flew unseen. Your suit might be able to seal such a puncture, but the thought of even a single three-millimeter dart punching clean through your body any place it chose could become distracting.

For all the frenzy of streaking suits and streaking missiles, the fight was already dying down. The Grinders had started out outnumbered. It was the inevitable arithmetic of any battle where all formation broke down. Here and there the more numerous force found two-to-one matches. Winning those, they now had two combatants free to tip the scales of two more single combats. The advantage spread exponentially, so that the fight might appear to hang in the balance for a while, then suddenly be decided in a few minutes. So that even as Arvada watched, the number of silver-flashing transponders riding the red streaks of exhaust through space engulfed, then smothered the others.

Still, it had been a costly business. Bodies drifted in profusion. Those of the Grinders had their heads pulped. But even the faces of some of the Marines, their suits breached beyond repair, lay hidden behind a paste of blood and lung tissue. They would have held their breath as long as they could, even while absolute zero and vacuum seared their flesh and burned out their eyes. But in the end, sixty or ninety seconds usually, suffocation would trigger the autonomous reflex to gasp for air. And then their lungs would burst outward.

"Sleds, move in. Those of you still able-bodied, collect the wounded first" — there wouldn't be many, not fighting in space — "and get them aboard the sleds from the *Keyna*. Then gather the dead and bring them to the other sleds. For now, they too shall be taken to the *Dysis* pending identification."

All these dead, just to get her hands on a holobrain.

"Sergeant Latumba," she called. "You and Corporal Trennan bring Beck to me. Marines from *Lyngheid*, assemble on me. We are going to ready the holobrain for transfer."

She looked around at the bodies drifting all about, trailing icy streamers from rents in their suits.

Let's hope it was worth it.

And let us also hope it provides the bridge to Sahan I need. The one I killed all these people for.

And most of all, let us hope that our love, tortured as it has sometimes been, can overcome the hate the Evolved have programmed into him.

#

About the Author

Richard Quarry writes science fiction, fantasy, crime, and historical adventure. His short fiction has appeared in *Fiction River* and *Blaze Ward Presents*. He lives in Seattle, where he enjoys hiking the hills and beaches of the Northwest with his wife Claire. Check out more of his books and stories at richardquarrywriter.com.

Grinder is the sixth book of *The Evolved Saga*. Please read on to see a sample from the saga's conclusion, *The God Machine*.

And if you enjoyed this story, please consider leaving a review. Thanks.

The God Machine

Chapter 1

THE HOLOBRAIN WAS AN awkward damn thing.

Arvada stood by while the Marines used cutting torches to free the mechanism from the shattered hull of the freighter. Around her floated dozens of dead Grinders. Sheets of ice formed from blood and ruptured body organs projected from rents in their silver suits. Within their helmets their heads were no more than pulp, because the Evolved had rigged them with explosives to burst when the suits detected vital signs falling below a certain threshold.

The Marines and Riggers she'd led into the battle to take the freighter had suffered their own casualties, but the last of the dead were even now being loaded aboard the landing craft to be taken back to the *Dysis*. The Peregrines had made fairly short work of the Grinders. But seventeen of them died during the free-wheeling battle in space.

Seventeen men and women who would still be alive if Arvada hadn't insisted on capturing the holobrain.

She didn't think much about it, now. She'd made a judgment. In war judgment involved casualties. Whether or not this particular judgment was justified could only be evaluated at some later date, when its overall effects could better be assessed. But whether or not, perfect wasn't an option. You did your best, fought hard, and kept your eyes pointed toward the future. As she was pointing hers now.

Later, in the night, it might be different. If so, she would face it then. As always.

The actual mass of brain tissue forming the holobrain followed a rough kidney shape, a little over a meter on the long side and two-thirds that in height. It rested within a fluid bath inside a transparent shell two meters in diameter.

Arvada's previous experience with the holobrains, along with that of the *Geniah* expedition three decades before, revealed that while the shell could be pierced by laser or super-speed drill, enabling nanoprobes to be inserted into the tissue, it was opaque to any electromagnetic transmission.

Yet it could somehow transmit a form of thought.

Not human thought, not at least in any manner that anyone other than Hypatia Wren and perhaps Sahan Kotori had ever been able to comprehend. And both their reputations would require significant upgrades just to reach controversial.

But the holobrains hosted, to greater or lesser degree depending on their internal complexity, an embodiment of the Group Mind. And this could communicate with the Living Evolved who oversaw the war against the Peregrine Alliance, and exert total control over the Grinders, who actually fought it.

Though the brain itself could survive indefinitely without external life support by entering some form of sporified state, in active operation it was fed by tubes from a whole array of fluids and filters, pumps and converters, cooling and heating mechanisms, and a variety of nutrients whose composition had been analyzed, but not their function.

Together these occupied about the same space and slightly more mass than a land-based personnel carrier. Either fire from the *Dysis* or the Grinders' efforts to sabotage the mechanism had fused parts of it into the ruptured hull. The support structure itself did not appear badly damaged, but Arvada wanted it whole and intact as possible. Should the holobrain be detached from its support mechanism, it would go on living, but form a core around its outer layers, deactivating itself.

So Arvada couldn't just order the Marines rip it loose. She needed it functioning. Or rather Beck, her Evolved prisoner, did.

Finally they cut it free and pushed it into space. One of the landing craft approached, gull-winged roof opening. The Marines guided it into the craft with small booster rockets.

Unfortunately, having lost her ship, Arvada had no place to put it. So she prevailed upon Solange O'Grady to store the holobrain on board the line of battle ship *Dysis* until Arvada could get another command of her own.

"You do go through them, don't you," was Solange's rather snide remark.

That could be a problem. As soon as the fleet left the Rione system, the site of the battle in which Arvada had led her force to victory over the traitor Raisa Catalan's Collaborationists, her official authority ended. The name Arvada Sattar carried a lot of *cachet* these days, hence her command of the task force. But that command, broadly agreed upon by the fleet, ended with the battle, leaving her in actual fact a Lieutenant

Commander addressing senior Captains. The most senior of whom was Solange O'Grady.

The holobrain would then in practice be under Solange O'Grady's control. She might assert her authority and declare the holobrain property of the fleet, to be examined by a broad-based team.

Arvada did not want the holobrain stored aboard the *Dysis*. That would do Beck absolutely no good at all. Unless he remained aboard the heavy, Solange's prisoner instead of Arvada's.

That was no good.

Arvada harbored not the slightest doubt about Solange's will to fight. But the fiery redhead's great passion was ship-to-ship, broadside-to-broadside combat. Admiral Nelson would have loved her. But that was not how Arvada had fought the war to this point. Not how she had scored her victories. Not how she believed the war would be won.

Not against the Evolved.

So she asked Solange — "ask" being all she could do now that the fleet had made their Jump from Rione — if they might have a little chat. Informally. Over coffee. Just girls together.

Chapter 2

He woke lying on his bunk. Frequently it took him a moment to remember where he was, in part because of the swirl of impressions, and partly because the narrow, over-firm bed and the gray steel bunk and walls marked so many of his domiciles. Not just in Navy life, but the Dainichi before. Only for them it had served as the "time-out" quarters — detention, really — where he whiled away so many happy hours.

He quickly oriented himself.

The pain reminded him.

He'd been a bad boy. Again.

He wasn't sure just how. Something to do with the Grinders? Something he'd been trying to tell them? Something they'd been trying to tell him?

We are one.

Had he said that? What had he meant? It was all very vague. Everything was vague. Except the bruises from beating himself against hard objects. Of course they weren't really there. This Grinder body, or rather the simulacrum of one the Evolved had given him, possessed neither the skin nor the flow of blood to leave bruises. The Evolved just liked to tweak his circuits from time to time, remind him that though his mind might live here, the house still belonged to them. And they could make him feel anything they damn well pleased.

Not that it was a whole lot of pain anyway. Just a stiff, bruised feeling in his ribs, arms, and legs. He could move them, but it took effort.

Which he found curious. Because some of this body was actual muscle, though artificially cultured, and some a high-tech pseudo-quantum mishmash on some matrix between steel, plastic, and organic tissue.

But not one molecule of it was his own. No more than any of the nerves or whatever served for them.

All that really remained to him was his brain. And Sahan had his suspicions about that. He knew that by stimulating pain in his brain the Evolved could cause excruciating agony that seemed to come from his own long-lost limbs. That much he'd tested empirically, more than even his generally skeptical nature required.

Of course a brain should not have pain receptors.

Just another little improvement the Evolved had thrown in.

But why leave behind this *bruised* sensation?

Not as a reminder to stay within established boundaries. The Evolved could remind him of anything they wanted anytime they pleased, and make it a lot harder to forget.

Not as punishment, either, for the same reason. It took a lot more than bruises and hunger to get Sahan's attention, as the Dainichi learned early.

Startled, Sahan rolled into a sitting position. He'd forgotten all about the Dainichi. Hadn't thought a thing about them for … a very long time. Couldn't, because there'd been nothing but a hole where they used to be.

So what were such memories doing in his head now?

The Evolved must want them there. Why else inflict this bruising sensation, no more than a minor irritant?

That had been his life with the Dainichi. Six, eight, eleven, fourteen years old. All through those years the pain stayed with him. Of course the Dainichi never beat him. They were against violence. But they did have something approaching reverence for Tai Chi, and Sahan loved knocking people into floors and walls in Push Hands. A little demented that way, he was.

So since it wasn't safe to put anyone his own age against him, they matched him against older, larger, more experienced opponents. Who in self-defense handled him roughly. Until about fourteen, when they couldn't handle him at all. Not even the instructors.

And so they launched him into outside bouts. Normally the Dainichi kept their own from Alliance matches, because they smacked of the abhorred "competition." But they hoped to humble the boy.

Didn't work. But it did keep up the pain.

Not that he minded. In fact he gloried in it. Wore it like a badge. His reward for pissing off the whole world, which while he couldn't at present remember the details, he was pretty sure he'd been really good at.

As for the pain, you could never make it disappear, but you could learn to set it to one side. Even use the pressure of it to intensify whatever else you set your mind to. He'd learned early to split his awareness into two parts, using the one to stimulate increased power in the other.

Why were these recollections coming to him now?

He ran his hands over his Grinder arms, his Grinder legs, his Grinder face. He still wasn't used to the way the fingers swung out over his mouth and jaws.

Funny thing, fate. In the end, this — *this* — really was his proper place, wasn't it? Enemy to all. Stripped of all the humanity many doubted he possessed in the first place. Even the Dainichi, who venerated humor the way people who seldom get the joke often do, would be falling all over themselves.

Well, he'd amassed a lot of pain and a lot of petty satisfaction. Then he met Arvada.

Smartest thing he ever did — that is, if it really was pain that made him feel the most satisfied.

Sahan held his hands up before him. Long, slender fingers striated as an anatomy book. Skeletal palms with an oily green-gold sheen.

Always going where none had gone before, that was Sahan Kotori.

So where do you go from here, little man?

Finish out the game.

Crash himself against the last, most irresistible pain life had offered him.

Arvada Sattar.

He called out to the Evolved.

"Did you really doubt? Was that why these memories? No need. I'll destroy Arvada for you. You people are into patterns, right? Well me and Arvada, this pattern is *ours*."

He settled back on the bunk.

All his life he'd been splitting himself down the middle. The search for love, and the search for pain.

Time to bring the two halves together.

www.ingramcontent.com/pod-product-compliance
Lightning Source LLC
Chambersburg PA
CBHW071459140726
47997CB00005B/1786